THE TROUBLE WITH TRYING TO LOVE A HELLION

MURDER SPREES & MUTE DECREES, BOOK THREE

JENNIFER CODY

Copyright © 2023 by Jennifer Cody

All rights reserved.

No part of this book may be reproduced in any form or by any electronic or mechanical means, including information storage and retrieval systems, without written permission from the author, except for the use of brief quotations in a book review.

Formatting by Tammy, Aspen Tree E.A.S.

Book Cover Design by Tammy, Aspen Tree E.A.S.

Editing by Shannon, Aspen Tree E.A.S.

NOTE FROM ROMILY

Hello my lovely readers! It is I, your beloved leader, Romily Butcher. We have to talk about a few things before you dive into my pupper's story.

First, no, I am not narrating this book. This is narrated by my new son, Edovard, and he is a beautiful boy with a wonderful heart; however, he does not read or write well, so this story was dictated, and we all know how awful dictation software can be.

Well, some of us do; others of us have never experienced it for obvious reasons.

So while my boy was dictating the story, his family was with him, and we might have made some comments that the software picked up. While we have had this book edited, we chose to keep the comments by the family in place, so occasionally you will come across some interjections to the story. Just go with it. It's fine.

Second, we're an inclusive family, and if Edovard was developmentally delayed, we would still love him, but I want to make it clear that he is not developmentally delayed in any way. My beautiful, soft, cinnabun pupper is simply at the other end of the spectrum from the cherubs. Some people are just not book smart, and Edovard isn't book smart, but that doesn't mean he isn't smart in other ways, and we value his insight about the things he knows a lot about.

He is an adorable soul and we love him. His narrative reflects his innocence and personality. This isn't the complex beautiful prose you get with my books (why are you laughing??); it's simpler and chock full of the wonder of a sweet summer child.

That's pretty much all I have to say about him.

Content issues! Basically, if you made it through the first two books, this one will be fine too. There is blood, gore, viscera...you know, the usual. There is a non-con dancefloor kiss that incites the usual amount of justice, and someone calls my pupper dumb, but that only serves to bring the family together in a special way (as only murder can).

Love from the bottom of my sassy, sunny heart,
Romily Butcher

PS: Here's the reading list from the last book:
Bee Cave Magic- Kelly Fox
Untouched- MA Innes
Dirty Forty- Mia Monroe

THE TROUBLE WITH TRYING TO LOVE A HELLION

The Roommate Arrangement- Saxon James
Bandit- Brook Matthews

CHAPTER 1

The air here is really hot compared to Fresno. It's like I'm getting baked in an oven like a chocolate vanilla swirl cupcake. Or one of those German chocolate cakes. Actually, I'm probably more like a gingerbread man.

Gosh I'm hungry.

We flew all the way to Arizona yesterday, and it's been at least two hours since breakfast, and now we're sitting in an arena like they used to build in the olden days when there were Roman emperors. Except there aren't any vendors trying to get me to spend eight dollars on a hot dog. I would, though, if there was.

My stomach rumbles as my new Oppa (that means "Dad"), Arlington Fox, shuffles his bare feet in the sand of the arena. It makes me wince because that sand is probably really hot.

I don't really want to look at what is going to happen—I get a little sick when I see people die, so I look away from Oppa and Bellamy (my new brother) to the crowded stands of the arena. There are a lot of people here to watch the guys who did bad things to Bellamy die. Papa (my other new dad, Romily Butcher) told me that we're making a statement to the community of supernatural people: Don't fuck with the Foxilys.

I'm a Foxily, or I will be when we all change our names. Fox says he needs to change his identity in the next five to ten years, and when he does, we are all getting new names. I haven't picked out a first name yet, but I'm excited about getting to be a Foxily. I like how it sounds, and it's nice to have a family again.

My eyes find the guy everyone keeps telling me is evil, but I've learned not to judge people before I get to know them. Look at me. I'm over six feet tall, I'm brown skinned, I have a square face, and I'm super buff. I like being a bodybuilder. I don't need to compete with anyone else; this is purely for fun, and people judge me by my looks all the time. They assume I'm some kind of tough guy, or a criminal, or whatever. I'm not. I'm just strong because I like being strong.

The blond curls on top of Santanos' head shine like a real halo, and the way his pretty blue eyes look at me makes me feel tingly sometimes. I don't know why everyone thinks he's evil. He's been nothing but nice to me. He saw how upset I was when my new dads were gone saving my new brother, and he gave me a cup of hot tea he said would relax me. It tasted like the tea my grandma used to drink before bed, so I know he was trying to help.

No one is going to convince me that a guy who gives a stranger hot tea like that is a bad guy.

The tingles are weird though. Never felt anything like that before.

"Here you go, baby boy."

One of my new grandfathers—I can't remember what I'm supposed to call them all yet; this one is blue—hands me a really big glass full of sparkling ice water.

I'm thirsty, so I smile gratefully at him. "Thank you, Grandpa."

His love for me shines out of him and he pats my head, telling me he's happy I'm a part of his family now.

I like how all the people in my new family let their love for me shine like they do. As long as they're with me, I'll never be alone in the dark again.

I chug about half the water, and when I look in the glass to see how much is left, it magically refills, which is pretty cool. I didn't know magic like this existed until recently, but some of the things that magic does are incredible. Like refilling my glass so I won't get dehydrated in Arizona's summer heat. All I ever knew about was just the stuff I could see, and I like knowing there's magic out there that I can't see.

The announcer guy starts telling us about the reason we're here today as my eyes catch on Santanos again, staring at me. There's a lot of light in him, too. He has a lot of love inside him; I can see it. I don't think it has anything to do with me, but I like looking at people who have lots of love inside them. My sister doesn't have any love inside her. She never has, especially not toward me.

I don't want to think about that right now.

I'd rather look at Santanos, because even though I don't judge people based on their looks, I do like how pretty he is. He's really nice to look at.

My other grandpa, who's sitting with Santanos, reaches over and smacks the back of his head. Santanos spins around to—um, I think that one is Dora, no Dorito? I can't remember. Some kind of D name I never heard before—and I can almost hear his loud protest at being smacked by my new grandpa. Almost. He has a really nice voice, and I kinda wish I could hear it again.

Instead, the announcer tells us that the executions can begin, and despite not really wanting to watch, I end up watching my Oppa and brother kill the people in the arena with them. It's kind of amazing, even if I get a little sick seeing the blood. I've never been around people who use swords like Oppa and Bellamy do. They're fast and strong and look like they're dancing as they kick up sand and turn it into reddish brown mud.

A lot of heads end up separated from their bodies, but I guess that's the point of this. Oppa and Bellamy are telling everyone not to mess with our family in the bloodiest way they could think of. Most of the people die fast, but two of them are left fighting after the others are killed.

One of them is a big lizard guy with a mohawk made up of spikes like rosebush thorns, but the spikes are made of bone instead of wood. He's got a long metal pole that he's using to defend himself against Bellamy. I've never seen anyone defeat one of the lizard people in a fight

(I saw a fight between a lizard person and a bird person once, and once I saw a lizard person win a fight against a sand person), but I trust Bellamy. He can defeat this one because he's a trained assassin, and I've watched him sparring with Oppa, and he's really good. Better than the lizard guy, that's for sure.

Oppa is fighting a really fast, mostly naked girl with long, black claws, wild messy hair that I think has a wasp nest in it, and a dark splotch on her chin like she's spilled so much grape juice while drinking that it's become a permanent stain. She looks ferocious, and she's fast enough that Oppa can't kill her right away.

Both Oppa and Bellamy fight fast and hard, and within just a few seconds of Bellamy cutting open the lizard guy's gut—the water I've drunk tries to make an escape, but I choke it back down and look away from the intestines—Oppa kills the wild girl by cutting off her claws and then her head.

It's so sad, and gross, and sad. I don't like watching people die.

I close my eyes to remove the sight, but instead of the usual red from behind my eyelids, I see the face of a person. That really startles me, because I don't ever see things when I close my eyes. That's why I close them. But this face. This guy is really dark, scary-dark. Dark like he has no love inside him at all.

"Seth Adam Hultgren. Thirty eight victims—no, no, no!" I cut off the weird words coming out of my mouth without my permission because it's really scary. "Papa!"

Papa is already in my lap and hugging me hard as tears start pouring down my face. I can't stop them from coming. I don't see faces; I don't randomly have names and stuff like that come spewing out of my mouth.

"Sshh, it's ok, baby boy," the blue grandpa says as he takes my hand and starts rubbing my back too. "That's just your Augur abilities kicking in. I guess they were waiting until the right time before they started up. You're ok. Now we have the name and a reason to investigate them. Did the magic tell you anything about the victims?"

I choke on my own tears. I knew I was supposed to be some kind of helper for Oppa, but it's been a couple weeks, and I haven't been at all helpful, except when he wanted some help clearing out one of the apartments next to our house (he's going to remodel it so that whenever me or Bellamy decide to move out of the main house we can just move in next door). Unfortunately, I do know more about the victims.

It's really hard to get the words out, but I manage to. "They're all dead. He killed a bunch of college girls from a university in Milwaukee."

All three of my new grandpas hiss at once, and then somehow Papa isn't in my lap anymore, and instead I'm looking at another blond, but this one has blue eyes instead of brown, and he looks pissed.

"What happened?" Santanos demands, putting his hands all over my face and shoulders and arms. It feels like he's touching me everywhere, and as soon as I realize that he basically wormed his way into my lap, the tingles start up again all over my body, especially where he's touching me.

"Why are you touching my son?" Papa's digital voice from his phone reads the words he writes aloud. I like it better when he lets one of the others read his words to me.

Santanos completely ignores my papa.

*"Stop feeling him up *exclamation point* He's just been through a traumatic event,"* the digital voice reads.

"I don't mind, Papa." It's kind of nice anyway. The tingles are a little fun.

"What happened?" Santanos repeats, this time looking me in the eye.

Weirdly, along with the light of his love that shines out from him, he smells like the smoke from the sage smudges my grandpa used to burn to help clean out his house.

"I guess I got my Augur powers," I explain, retelling him the information that my blue grandpa said. "Seth Adam Hultgren. He killed a lot of college girls in Milwaukee."

The light inside him dims. "Then I guess it's about time for Fox to make a trip to Wisconsin."

Oh. He never takes me out when he's working, but since he'll be going to a different state, I wonder if he'll take me too. Though I don't know if I want to go if we're just going there to kill someone.

"I've never been to Wisconsin. Is it nice there?" I think I should get more information before I decide if I want to go to a different place.

Santanos' hands stop moving, and one of them holds my neck and he presses the other over my racing heart. "It's nice. Very mid-American. There's some famous breweries there. Do you like beer?"

I shake my head. "I don't really like alcohol, and beer tastes bad."

Santanos' light brightens again when he laughs and pats my chest. "It is certainly an acquired taste."

One second Santanos is there in my lap and the next he's gone, and there's a bunch of fighting, and then a gun goes off and Oppa is suddenly here with blood spurting out of his neck from a gunshot wound, and then my grandfathers all attack one of the people that I've seen with Santanos, and it's all just so bad!

"Stop fighting!" I yell, standing up and grabbing Santanos out of the mess of bloody bodies. How did they all get so bloody so fast?

Bellamy lets out a loud, painful whistle (not sure how he got here so fast), and that stops everyone except my Oppa, who can't just stop bleeding (he'll be ok because he heals really fast). "Family meeting, now!" my new brother yells, getting everyone's attention. "Edovard, why don't you just hold on to Santanos for a minute and keep him nice and safe while I talk to the dads and grandads."

I nod and pull Santanos closer, hugging him so he's safe.

The dads and grandparents all move together off to the side and start whispering to each other, and Santanos' friend that is always around, the big guy who looks kind of Chinese, comes and stands in front of me, staring at me with a mean look. He's got a little love in him, but mostly he's kind of dark and gray.

Santanos moves in my arms and wraps me up in his arms and legs. "Full body hugs are my favorite," he says, pushing his face into my neck.

Those words make me really happy. "Mine too. My grandma used to give the best hugs."

"I never had a grandma I was close to. My mom, however, she's one of the queens of Hell, is an excellent hugger when she deigns to give one."

"Hell? Like the bad place?" I ask, a little scared by that.

Santanos hugs me a little tighter and kisses my neck to comfort me. "It's not really a bad place. It's just a place like any other. The dirt is red there, but that's just because there is more iron oxide than usual in it. We have a booming iron and steel industry in Hell. Most magical weapons are made by demon hands."

"Oh, I thought Hell was the place bad people go."

Santanos chuckles, tickling my neck with his breath. "The afterlife isn't one of my areas of expertise. Whatever happens after people die happens. It's none of my business."

Before I know what to say to that, my family breaks apart and turns toward me with my blue grandpa in front.

"Ok, Edovard, as a family we'd like to know if you want to stay home, go to Milwaukee with your dads and brother, or come stay with me and your grandpas while they're killing the guy in Milwaukee."

Santanos takes his face out of my neck. "You can also come stay with me while they're gone, or I can go to Milwaukee with you and show you around town while they're working."

Oppa steps out in front of my blue grandpa. "He's not ever staying with you."

Santanos' face gets mean when he looks at Oppa. "He's welcome in my home."

Papa's digital voice says, *"I have seen the ceiling in your bedroom and that would traumatize my kid. You are not bringing him to your home, ever. You want to see him, you see him at our house."*

Oppa and Papa stare at each other for a second, then Oppa turns back to Santanos. "You can get through the ward as long as you have no plans to harm me or any member of my family."

Santanos turns his pretty face back to me. "Do you want me to come visit you? I can stay with you when the others go to Milwaukee if you don't want to go with them."

My stomach growls, and I really just want to get something to eat, so I just blurt out the first thing that comes to mind. "We can all go to Milwaukee together."

My blue grandpa huffs and spins away. "I hate Milwaukee."

"You don't have to go," Santanos calls after him.

"Like I would leave you alone with my baby boy!" he yells back.

"I'm really hungry. Can we stop fighting now?" I say, sad because no one likes Santanos even though he's so nice.

Santanos pets my shoulder. "Of course, sweetie. How does curry sound?"

I shrug. "I never had it."

"You're in for a treat, then." He whistles as he jumps out of my arms. "We're getting curry. We'll meet you at the restaurant. Objections can be filed with the objections manager." He points toward a wall where there's a trashcan but not anyone who might be a manager. I can usually see everyone in a room even when some people can't see them, so I'm a little confused about where the objections manager went before I looked, but I don't have time to ask because Santanos tugs me along with him inside the arena.

"Bellamy, keep an eye out for a text from Hassan for the address."

<Papa: Why does Hassan have your phone number?

Bellamy: That is an excellent question.

Gregory: The depot updates our phones every time you change your number.

Bellamy: How did I forget about that?

Papa: Rather irresponsible of you, don't you think?

Bellamy: I notice you didn't say anything every time we changed my phone number...>

CHAPTER 2

"Maybe we shouldn't have dinner with everyone in the same place." The Indian restaurant is kind of small, and I don't know if we'll all fit inside it. I count on my fingers how many of us there are, but I lose track because I can't remember my grandpa's names, so I shrug. "There's a lot of us."

Plus they don't like Santanos, and that's just hard for me to have to deal with. It makes me tired sometimes.

"There's only ten of us, sweetie. We can just push a couple of tables together," Santanos says, and his Chinese friend decides to show me how to push tables together.

<Papa: Are you actually Chinese?

Hassan: Mongolian.

Papa: Good job, pupper!

Hassan: I would have corrected him the first time if I needed to.>

I know how to push tables together, so I help him. He doesn't seem to like me much, and he scowls at me when I scooch the tables together as soon as he moves the chairs. I don't understand why everyone is so hateful. It seems like life is a little bit better when people just keep their love in their heart.

"Do you like your life?" I ask Santanos, because he's full of love, so hopefully that means he likes his life.

He smiles and steps in close, looking up at me. He's smaller than me, and I like the way he's making me feel like a giant. It's kind of fun to pretend.

"I enjoy my life. I believe in my job, and even though I never thought of myself as evil, I do a good job as the Avatar of Evil. I like being part of keeping the balance, and we are working toward balancing things out better."

His voice makes me feel like a kitten is purring on my chest. It's a really nice feeling, and that's another reason why I know Santanos isn't evil. He makes me feel good every time I'm around him just by talking. I don't get why anyone would think he's a bad guy. Although I probably should ask what his job is.

"What does avatar mean?" I whisper to my phone's dictionary app. I have two dictionaries, the big one, and then sometimes I need the little one to help me understand the big one. Ok, it's a kid's dictionary app, and it really does help me when the regular dictionary uses big words to define the other big words.

The big dictionary starts talking about Hindu gods, and I know Santanos isn't one of those, so I cut it off really quickly because the digital voice is pretty loud in the quiet restaurant.

Santanos' friend snorts. "It's a person who is given the power to represent an idea. In this case, Santanos is the Avatar of Evil. Inside of him is the power to be the boss of every person who's evil. He is the living, breathing embodiment of the concept of evil. That doesn't mean he is evil; he just rules over it."

I press my lips together and try to figure out what embodiment means, but Santanos' friend must be really smart because he says, "When you give something that doesn't usually have a body a body, that is when you embody it."

"Like if I didn't have a body, and then you made one for my soul, then I would be embodied?" That feels like a stretch, but I am trying to understand.

"Exactly like that," the dude grunts.

Santanos pats the guy's abs with a smile and then pulls out a chair. "Edovard, sit here and I will sit in your lap, ok?"

Since he was nice enough to pull my chair out for me, I sit in it. "Ok," I say, so he knows it's ok to spend time in my lap.

Santanos sits on my legs crossways, and his friend sits next to me. And then the three of us are sitting at a table for ten, and I don't know if anyone told my family where to meet us.

"Did you tell Bellamy where to meet us?"

Santanos picks up the menu in front of me as his friend tells the server that we want water for the table, and then he tells me, "I messaged them the address when we arrived. They should be here shortly."

That's good. Probably. Well, hopefully. Hopefully no one gets into another fight.

"So, if you're the ruler of all the evil people, why don't you just tell them not to be evil?" I ask, because I know he's good and good people don't like evil people, right?

"I can do a lot of things, but I can't tell evil people to stop being evil. Besides, the world would be boring without the antagonists in it. Humans especially need people to challenge them to be better." He points to a picture on the menu, showing it to me. "This is seven curry. It's a great way to try different types of curries to figure out what kinds you might like. I'm getting it for you unless you have objections."

I'm not a lawyer, and why would a lawyer call out an objection about food? What would a judge say about that? Is curry against the law?

No, it can't be, because we're in a whole restaurant for curry. I'll look that word up later because I think I might not understand what it means when he says it like this, but right now I can just tell him, "I'd like to try it. But is it a lot of food? Because I'm pretty hungry."

Santanos smiles at me with his teeth and the crinkles around his eyes make me tingly again. "I'll make sure there's enough food to fill you up, sweetie. We'll get plenty of appetizers for the table, so you can have as much as you want."

"As much as I want?" I almost can't believe he said that, because the only time I ever used to get as much as I wanted was when I bought my own food. I always had to share all the food my grandma made and she only gave me as much as she gave my grandpa. I always felt like I could eat both of our plates if he ever didn't like his dinner (he always liked it).

"Of course. You're so big, we have to feed that body so you can maintain it, don't we?"

I smile because I know all about maintenance and gains too. I know about my body and how to take care of it. I've worked really hard to learn all about body-building and nutrition stuff. "It does take a lot of food to keep up with my metabolism, especially when I'm trying to grow. I haven't found the right gym for me yet, and I don't have a job yet, but when I get one, I'm going to find a really good gym and get back to my workout schedule."

The bell above the door jingles while I'm talking, and my family starts walking in, but Santanos doesn't let them interrupt our conversation.

"I own a gym. Hassan here uses it. We would be delighted to give you a tour," he offers.

"You're the nicest person I've met besides my family," I tell him and hug him to my chest. "I'm really glad I met you," I mumble into his tickly hair.

"Why is it every time I leave you alone with my son you end up on his lap?" Papa asks, using Bellamy to read his words.

Santanos snuggles into my arms more and relaxes, letting his love shine out of him. "My ass is the most perfect ass in all of creation and deserves to rest on the most perfect seat in all of creation."

Wow. I didn't know Santanos had the most perfect bottom. I clench my hands around his waist and almost lift him up so I can see, but I stop myself just in time. I almost forgot to ask.

I lean back, trying to see his butt, but since he's sitting, it's hard. "Can I see?" I ask, almost lifting him up before he can answer.

I'm way too excited that the perfect butt is sitting on me. It's cool, though, right? Who else can say they've had the perfect butt in their lap? Well, I guess everyone who's ever had Santanos in their lap. I wonder if Hassan gets to be Santanos' seat sometimes too?

"You are not ogling Santanos' butt in front of the family," the blue grandpa says quickly, but Santanos is already standing up and sort of bending over the table, which gives me the best view of his perfection.

"Wow." I think that is the perfect butt. It's really round...and my mouth is watering.

I swallow the extra saliva and glance toward the bathroom. I don't think it smells that good in here, so maybe I'm about to get sick. My mouth always waters before I have to throw up, which sucks because I was really happy being Santanos' seat.

I glance at Hassan again and reluctantly point to Santanos' perfect butt. "You should probably let him sit on your lap, dude. I'm feeling a little weird."

Oppa, who walked around the table to sit next to me, pushes Santanos toward Hassan without a word, but Papa's digital voice talks for Oppa.

"You heard my son, go sit on your lackey's lap."

"How are you able to push me?" Santanos questions, moving Hassan over and sitting in his chair next to me.

Oppa grunts, and the grandpa with the D name laughs. "It's all about his intentions and temperance. If he's not actively trying to harm you and is being careful not to accidentally hurt you, your ward isn't going to activate."

I lean over to Oppa and whisper really quietly. "I forgot the grandpa's names again."

He puts his arm around my back and leans close to my ear to whisper back. "That one is Dakota, you can call him Grandpa D. The blue one is Grandpa Tag. Grandpa Amos is right next to him, and the one who looks like Thor is Grandpa Bear."

That's probably why I keep forgetting his name; he doesn't want me to call him by it. "Thank you for telling me again."

I give him a side hug because he likes hugs from me, and then the waiter comes over and everyone starts ordering drinks, and then Santanos orders a bunch of appetizers and the blue grandpa—Grandpa Ta–n? Tag. Right, tag like the game. Grandpa Tag frowns at Santanos. "I don't think we need that many appetizers."

Santanos is so pretty, even when he smiles like a movie villain. I guess I can see why people think he's evil even though he's definitely not. "I didn't order any appetizers for you."

I reach over and take his hand, pulling his eyes back to me. "It's ok if we share, Santanos. Sharing can be fun too, you know."

He smiles at me and pats my cheek. "Ok. Just because you said so."

His love brightens again, so I know he really likes sharing too, and I turn back to Grandpa Tag. "We're going to share our appetizers. Santanos says there will be plenty of food, so everyone will get as much as they want."

Grandpa Tag reaches across the table and ruffles my hair up. "You're such a good boy, Edovard. I'm so glad you joined our family."

I am too, even though they're all a little bit, um, violent.

CHAPTER 3

I think curry is my new favorite food. There are so many different kinds and I really like them all. And Santanos was right, there was enough that I got to have as much as I wanted. I am so full, but it was hard to stop eating when it was all so good.

I try not to make a fuss about my stomach, but I think Santanos might be a mind reader, because when we get back in his limo after supper, he pulls my head into his lap so I can lay down since I made myself feel gross. It was worth it, though.

"That was so good." If that sounds like a complaint, it's only because my stomach hurts.

"You ate more than you should have," he chuckles, running his fingers through my hair.

I shrug and close my eyes because it feels good, like when my grandma used to do it when I needed a nap. I needed a lot of naps when I was growing up, but she always made it nice to fall asleep when I thought I should be playing instead.

I yawn, but I don't want to fall asleep in the car, so I try to think of something to say. "Do you know anyone who would hire someone like me? I was working at a gas station, but Papa kidnapped me from there, and I lost my job."

"Why do you need a job?" His voice is so soothing, it makes me yawn again.

"Because (yawn) I have to be able to (yawn) pay for a gym and clothes and stuff."

"You get paid for being an Augur. You don't have to get another job."

"No, I told them to give that to Papa or Oppa. I looked up the cost of living here because my grandma told me that I needed to find out how much it cost to live somewhere before I moved, and since I moved here I had to look it up. It's so expensive, so I just told them to give my Augur payments to the Foxilys to cover the cost of my rent and food. Oppa said he'll make sure it gets to the right IRA for me. I don't know what that is, but he said it was important for when we decide to stop working for my grand-sugar-daddy." She's really nice. She gave me a bunch of workout shirts. They say nice things on them, and I'm looking forward to wearing them to the gym.

"I see. So you want to work in addition to being an Augur. You're going to have to work for someone who understands that you can't control your Augur abilities and that you're going to have to put them first," he says softly, and it makes me yawn again.

"Yeah. Do you know anyone like that?" I close my eyes because it's hard to fight against how tired I am.

"You can work for me."

<Grand Sugar Daddy: That's how he got my baby??? That is cheating!

Santanos: Avatar. Of. EVIL.

Grand Sugar Daddy: I will get my revenge.>

HIKING up a mountain is hard enough without having to drag a boulder up with me. I don't know why I have to take the boulder up to the top of the mountain; I just know it's my job to get it up there. Every time I take a step, the boulder tries to drag me back. It's so hard. Why did I agree to take this boulder up to the top? Who even asked me to do this? I'm strong, but I'm barely strong enough for this, and it's going to take me forever.

I guess I could try to push it instead of pull it.

I try to get behind it, but the boulder slides down the mountain every time I take a step to get behind it. Frustration makes my heart angry. I hate this boulder!

I groan, pulling myself out of that awful dream. I hate dreams like that. No one wants to wake up on the wrong side of the bed, and those dreams always make my mornings the worst.

I take a deep breath as my body wakes up, and I notice the warm body in front of me. I'm spooning someone. They smell nice. Like sage—oh.

I open my eyes and discover a halo of pretty blond hair under my nose. I'm snuggling Santanos. That's nice. I wonder how I got into a bed with him...

And Hassan?

Santanos' friend is snuggling Santanos on the other side of him.

Awww, they're so cute. Hassan is holding Santanos' hand and their foreheads are pressed together. Hassan's usually dark insides are calm and glowing happily. He must really love Santanos. I like seeing that.

I wish I could lay here with them, but my mouth tastes bad and I really need to pee, so I gently pull my arm out from under Santanos, and roll away—

Right into someone else, who grunts and startles awake with a yelp.

His noise wakes everyone up, and when he sits up, he glares at me with a lot of darkness inside him. There's a little bit of love inside him, not more than I thought was in Hassan, and it's definitely not like Santanos.

"What the hell?" he gripes, throwing off the blanket wrapped around his naked body.

I want to close my eyes and not stare, but my eyebrows think they should be part of my head hair and won't let me close my eyes. "Why are you naked?" I ask, trying not to stare at his—little guy. It's poking straight out. "Are you ok?" Maybe his little guy is broken and that's why he's angry?

"Gregory," Santanos moans, turning over and curling over me, resting his head on my chest. For some reason, he's also naked. "Why did you wake us up?"

"Because your behemoth decided to squish me," Gregory yells, pointing at me.

Santanos' head shoots up, but I stroke his hair like he did mine yesterday to calm him, because it's ok. Gregory isn't being mean to me on purpose. He's just grumpy and needs a lot more love in his heart. Maybe I can give him some love. "Gregory, those are hurtful words. We don't use our words to be mean to our friends, and since you're Santanos' friend you're my friend too. It's ok to be grouchy when someone wakes you up before you're ready. It's not ok to be mean to them when it was an accident. I'm sorry I accidentally woke you up. Now you say you're sorry for using hurtful words." Some people never learned how to apologize, and Gregory doesn't seem like anyone ever told him how to do it.

Gregory's mouth looks like an O as he stares at me, so I pat the bed beside me and open my arms. I really have to pee, but making sure he's ok is important. "Come here. You can cuddle in with Santanos while you find the right words."

Santanos pats the bed where I did, and Hassan lifts my arm that's holding Santanos, and he spoons in behind Santanos, and now it would just be weird for Gregory not to join the puppy pile, so he gives in with a huff and comes to snuggle me and Santanos.

<Papa: This is not how I imagined this morning going for my pupper...

Bellamy: I expected him to be a little more disoriented.

Me: I liked waking up with other people.

Santanos: I told you he would want to be with me.

Oppa: You literally snuck him into your hotel room and then called the human police to keep us from collecting him.

Santanos: Avatar of EVIL.>

As soon as he's settled in, I stroke his back to make sure he knows he's loved. "There, there."

Gregory snorts and Santanos laughs and turns his head so he can see me. His smile is so bright and happy even though he still looks sleepy and there are red lines on his face from his pillow (which was my arm). "Why did you just 'there, there' him?" he giggles out.

I pat Gregory gently on the butt even though he's naked. I think it's ok, but if it's not, he'll tell me to stop. Hopefully he doesn't because I know it's going to make him feel better. "My grandma always said 'there, there' when she was trying to make me feel better when I was upset. Butt pats and 'there, theres' are the best cure for grumpy guts."

"Grumpy guts," Santanos repeats, and for some reason Gregory laughs.

I smile at his happier mood and pat his butt again. I knew it would work. "Yes, because our grumpies start in our guts, so we just pat them out."

"I can't wait to introduce you to my people," Santanos decides, shining with love and happiness inside him.

<Bellamy: Makes sense to me.
Papa: This is the reason.
Me: What reason?
Papa: The reason that you belong in our family.>

"You're so pretty when you're happy," I sigh. "When do I get to meet your family?"

Hassan lifts his head and gives me a weird look, but the contentment inside him is still glowing a soft pink, so I don't think I've upset him. "Why would you want to meet Santanos' family?"

"Because they're important to him, and he said he wants to introduce me." Duh. Even I know what it means when someone talks about their people.

We all have our people, and my people are my new family, and maybe if Santanos wants, he can become part of my people too. I'd like to be family with him. He's so full of love that anyone would want to be part of his family.

"You want to meet one of the queens of Hell?" Gregory asks, looking at me wide-eyed.

"And a prince of Hell. Don't forget Bacchus," Hassan points out.

"Pshh. I know Hell isn't that scary. Santanos told me Hell makes magic weapons. It's not the bad place." They're trying to trick me into being scared, but I'm not going to let them. Santanos wouldn't lie to me.

"Can I please be there when you introduce him to Lilith?" Gregory begs. He really wants to be there, and it's nice that he wants to support me like that.

I pat his butt again and kiss the top of his head. "Thank you, Gregory. I would really like that."

Santanos' big blue eyes look a little worried, so I lean down and kiss the top of his head too. "Don't worry. Even if your parents don't like me, I will still like you." I squish everyone in a hug, which reminds me that I really need to pee, so I let them go. "I really need the bathroom now."

Gregory groans, but he rolls away off the bed, and Santanos lets me go and curls up with Hassan again, and as I walk to the hotel's bathroom, I glance behind to see Gregory scoot in with Santanos and Hassan, and I smile because it's nice when people love each other, and those three are full of love for each other. Well, Santanos is, and Gregory and Hassan also love him and each other in their own ways, even if they aren't full of love yet.

As I pull the front of my pants down to relieve myself, I decide that I am going to work really hard to help them fill up their lives with love so that their hearts can be full of it too. Everyone would be happier and the world would be a better place to live in if more people just let themselves love others.

Huh?

I think my little guy is looking a little bit bigger today. I wonder if curry makes people's penises get bigger. I know there's a lot of stuff out there that other people use that can affect their private parts, but I never heard of anything that really worked to make a penis bigger. Maybe I should ask Santanos—when I get him alone, because I'm not talking about my little guy in front of Gregory when his is broken or something. That would be pretty rude.

CHAPTER 4

I hold up the dirty pants I wore yesterday and all night and wonder if I should put them back on. They're pretty dirty, and I just showered, but I don't know if my luggage is here or not since I don't remember arriving. I fell asleep in Santanos' car and woke up here, so anything could have happened while I was asleep. Thankfully Santanos is nice and took care of me.

He'd probably be upset if I put on my dirty clothes and he went to the trouble of getting my luggage from the room I was supposed to share with Bellamy. I'll just fold these up, and if he didn't think of that, they'll still be here when I get done asking.

I wrap my towel around my hips and make sure it's very secure before leaving the bathroom. Too many comments in the gym's locker room have taught me to make sure my towel won't fall off. For some reason, a lot of guys kept calling me a monster, and I don't want to hear that from Santanos. I think that would hurt my feelings more than the comments from the random guys at the gym.

I head back to the bedroom, where Santanos is still cuddling with his friends. Well, no, that's not cuddling. Well, maybe it's exercise-cuddling. Hassan is behind Gregory, bumping into him with his hips, and they're both naked, and Santanos is watching. No, he's more than just watching.

There's a stream of light and happy love flowing out of Gregory and Hassan and into Santanos. It's making him brighter, but it's dimming the love that Hassan and Gregory have.

"Stop! Stop doing that! You're hurting yourselves!" I yell, running to separate them.

They both freeze, looking at me like I'm—well, they're looking at me like my teachers used to look at me when I would interrupt their lessons. I stopped interrupting their lessons, but I'm not wrong about this.

The light is almost completely gone from Gregory, so I grab him up and hug him tight and pat his butt. "Ssh. There, there. It's ok. I won't let them hurt you anymore."

I can't believe Santanos was stealing the tiny amount of love he had left in him, and I tell him so with a look that tells him he's hurting me. "You can't just steal people's love right out of them, Santanos."

Gregory is tense in my arms, so I pat his butt more firmly and rock him.

Hassan snorts, which draws my attention to the fact that his little guy is suffering the same condition that Gregory's is.

I frown at him too. "Gregory's almost completely out of love. You have more, but only a little bit more. Santanos was stealing it from both of you. That's why you're so grumpy. That's why you're both so grumpy."

"It's our job to give him our *love*," Gregory mumbles. He's not so tense since I started taking care of him, and when I look, he's much less dark, though that tiny spark of light in him is still barely glowing.

I give Santanos my grandma's most disappointed face. "You can't hire people to love you, Santanos. That's not how it works. You have to give them your love and then they love you back. You can't just pay someone to love you."

The look on Santanos' face tells me that he doesn't agree with me. "Edovard, I know this might not make sense to you, but I wasn't stealing their love. I was feeding myself. You interrupted my breakfast, sweetie. I pay them to feed me, and in order to do that, they have to engage in amorous activities."

I know I'm not the smartest person, and sometimes people say things that don't make sense right away, so I have to really think about them, but I don't know what he means and I'm too upset about Gregory's love almost winking out, so, "I can't talk to you right now. I'm taking Gregory to the other room and I'm going to make sure he's ok, and when I've calmed down we can have a talk about what we're going to do about you almost killing his heart. And I need you to think about how you're going to fix this, because I'm not going to let you keep taking his love out of him even if you're paying for it. You have to find a better way to get whatever it is that you need."

That's all I have to say about that, so I turn around and take Gregory to the sofa in the big room and sit with him on my lap, just stewing in my anger and patting his butt, hoping that will help fix him.

"You really didn't need to save me," he grumps.

I pat his butt harder because he seems to like that. "Be quiet and soak up my love. Yours is all messed up."

Gregory grumbles again but relaxes and lets me take care of him. Poor guy. Broken penis and now a blackened heart. He's having a rough day.

<Papa: This explains so much about you.

Gregory: I always wondered why I hated you right from the start. Now I realize it's because—

Papa: You have a cold dead heart?

Gregory: You're a nuisance.

Bellamy: Hassan. How's your neck?>

I DON'T KNOW how long I sit there with Gregory before Santanos and Hassan come out of the bedroom. Santanos is fine, but Hassan's light is even less bright than it was when I left, so I shoot Santanos a dirty look so he knows I know he didn't think about what I told him to.

One of his eyebrows rises up like Grandpa Tag's does sometimes when he thinks one of the other grandpas is being ridiculous, but I know I'm right and he's not going to change my mind. He can't just take

Gregory and Hassan's love right out of them until they don't have any more to give. It's not right.

"You look cozy," Santanos says, like he might be upset that Gregory needs attention, and he really should be, so I give him a softer frown instead of the mean stare I started with.

"He's all wrecked on the inside. You took almost all his love, so I'm trying to let him soak up a little of mine. It's working, and if you take it out of him again, I'm going to be very angry with you."

Gregory stirs and sits up, blinking at us like he's just waking up, though he wasn't really asleep; he just got into the zone of cuddles. "Can I get up now?"

I frown at his core, but it's looking better, and maybe it looks even better than it did when he woke up, so I nod and then pat my lap, looking at Santanos. We have to talk about what he did. "Let's make a plan for how to fix this for the next time."

That's what my grandma would have said. Sometimes I miss her.

Santanos smiles brightly and his love shines out of him, almost like it's reaching for me the same way he does as he sits in my lap. I like that he likes to sit close to me. It's nice to be wanted in his space even if I'm a little bit mad at him.

"Ok, sweetie, I think we need to discuss what I pay Hassan and Gregory to do for me and my needs, and then I need you to tell me what exactly you see when I use my magic so I can help you understand what I'm doing, because Gregory and Hassan have been with me for nearly a century and I have never gotten close to killing them."

His words are honest, he really believes that, and maybe it's true that he hasn't killed their bodies, but the love inside them is so dark it's almost dead and that's—well, that might be worse. A life without love in it isn't a very good life, is it?

I take a deep breath and try to say what I think my grandma would say. "Ok, Santanos. Thank you for thinking about some of the things I asked you to think about. I like that you came up with a plan. Why don't you start?" I think my grandma would be proud of me for that.

Santanos kisses my cheek with a kind smile and nods. "Gregory and Hassan are my bodyguards. I am one of the original four spawn of Lilith and Bacchus, who are important demons in Hell. Very powerful demons. Me and my siblings are called the Incubacchus because we get our main source of magical and mechanical sustenance from the living energy produced when people engage in intercourse."

I sigh, disappointed in myself because my grandma would understand him, but he's using a lot of big words and I don't always understand when people do that. Like right now. "I think I need my phone for this conversation," I confess, looking up at Hassan, who's just standing there watching us.

Santanos puts his hand on my cheek and pulls my face to look at him again. "I'm sorry. Let me explain that better for you. I'm a sex demon and I need people to have sex around me and with me or I will starve to death and die. Fortunately for me, people really like to have sex. I pay Gregory and Hassan to perform sex acts so that I can have the energy they produce to protect me and them. They're my bodyguards, and they make sure I am filled up and overflowing with power at all times."

Bellamy explained sex to me, but I guess it's different hearing about it than it is seeing it. I would not have guessed that Gregory and Hassan were sexing when I walked in. I didn't see much anyway because of the way Santanos was eating them.

"Ooooh." I'm so dumb. "I forgot that penises stand up like that to show that men want to sex. I thought Gregory had broken his penis." I laugh at myself. "Well, that's one less worry."

Gregory chokes on the drink he found and looks at me with shocked gray eyes. "You forgot what an erection is?"

"That's the word." I remember Bellamy telling me about them. "Yours is the first one I've ever seen, so I think it's fine that I forgot."

Gregory and Hassan both get really loud all of the sudden and it startles me, but Santanos hugs me tight and that helps me see that they're not mad at me; they're mad *for* me for some reason.

"What do you mean you've never seen an erection?" Gregory demands, and at the same time Hassan angry-asks, "You don't get erections?"

I look between them and then at Santanos, who looks curious, but not angry like Gregory and Hassan, so I just tell him what I told

Bellamy. "I've never wanted to sex, so I've never gotten an erection. Bellamy said it's ok. He said there are a lot of people who don't want sex. I think I'd be ok with it, but it's not something that's ever come up." I think about that for a second, just to make sure that I'm not lying, but I don't think I am. So I nod and shrug. "Papa says that I'll know if I'm ever ready to sex. He said that I might need a special person who makes me want to sex them, but he made sure to tell me that even if I don't ever want sex, that's fine too."

Well, except that means that I can't help feed Santanos, and I don't want him to be hungry. But Bellamy and Papa explained all about different sexualities and told me that I might fall under the a-sex—um, the a—uh…what's that word? A-something sexuality.

<Papa: Asexual or ace.

Me: Right, that's the word. Thanks.>

It's pretty complicated and there are a lot of different ways people can be ace, but since I've never wanted to sex, I'm probably asexual.

I examine Gregory's dim core and Hassan's angry core, and grimace. "Maybe it's not fine."

Gregory scoffs. "You're damn right, it's not fine."

Santanos raises a hand and that makes Gregory close his mouth.

I frown at him. "Gregory, it's ok if I don't want sex. A lot of people don't want sex, and that's ok. We don't tell people that the things they want are not ok. If you want people not to judge your sex, then don't judge theirs."

Hassan's core of magic brightens a bit, and Gregory's nearly blinks out. For a second I think I've accidentally made him lose all his hope and love, but then it winks back to life and it's just as bright as Hassan's, which is a huge relief.

I turn back to Santanos. "Gregory is better now, but you can't have his love any more today. He needs to work on getting it bright enough that when he gives it to you, it doesn't hurt him. That should be a rule for everyone. You can't take enough from anyone to hurt their cores."

Santanos leans his forehead against mine and closes his eyes. His love shines so bright that I almost don't even notice that he's taking some of mine. I do notice the tingles, though. That's probably why I see the little bit of love he's taking out of me because it feels tickly and tingly when he does it. I don't mind, but, "We ask before we take someone else's things," I remind him.

He laughs. "Sweetie, I'm not *taking* anything. You're the one shoving food in my face."

I look down at the flow of love between us. I guess he's right. It looks like I'm pushing my love into him. "Sorry. I guess I was trying so hard to fill Gregory up I forgot to stop." I've got way more love and light inside me than most people. Occasionally I'll see people with as much as me—Santanos is one of them, my grandma was one, there've been some others. I have enough to keep Santanos bright if he needs it to live. I'm happy to share—maybe I should have asked before sharing though. "Do you want me to stop?"

"I want you to stop when you're ready to stop. You made the new rule, and you're going to have to enforce it, because I can feel when Hassan and Gregory have given as much as they can, but I can't see the difference between as much as they can and a non-harmful amount like you can."

I think about that for a minute and decide that if he can't see the damage he's doing like I can, then he can't really be blamed for not knowing that he's killing their love. "I can do that. I can make sure you don't take too much, but you're going to have to give Hassan and Gregory time to recover because they're really dark right now."

Gregory glares at me. "I'm evil; of course I'm dark."

They keep telling me they're evil, so I guess I should stop trying to convince them that they aren't and just accept that they want to be evil. Maybe it's like what Papa said about the sex stuff. He said, we don't shame people for what they like. So I guess if they like to call themselves evil, I shouldn't try to fix that.

"Santanos is evil and he's as full of love as I am. He's as bright as, um, the lights at the gym. You can see everything at the gym and there's hardly any shadows. That's what his core looks like. We're going to try to get you back to full brightness too, that way you can be the best evil person you can be." There. That sounds exactly like something Papa would approve of.

Hassan's core brightens a teeny tiny amount, and I take that to mean that he appreciates me accepting their evilness, and that makes me happy.

"I will let Hassan and Gregory recover, but that means you're going to have to feed me, you know. Let's just call your job title, The Avatar of Evil's Assistant, and that way it covers any kind of work we decide you can do. Feeding me, helping my minions to be their best selves. I think having you as part of our organization is going to improve the quality of our lives."

"If nothing else, it'll improve the view," Gregory grumps, which is funny because that's a compliment, right?

<Gregory: I am allowed to think he's sexy!
Bellamy: No one was judging you.
Papa: Well...
Bellamy: You think he's sexy too.
Papa: I'm allowed to think hot people are hot.
Gregory: But I'm not?
Papa: This feels like a trap.>

I can't help how my heart fills up with love for Santanos, and I guess it sort of floods out of me into him, because his head falls back and his mouth drops open and he makes a noise that sounds like a moan but more breathy. The pull of the extra love out of me into him makes my entire body tingle and break out in goosebumps.

A shiver makes me squirm and hold him a little tighter, which makes the flood of love open up wider because I really, really like how loving him makes me feel.

Santanos wiggles on my lap, and the tingles turn into a shock of something that's so good it's a little scary, especially because it starts in my penis. That's new and scary but nice, and maybe I need to stop the flow because it's starting to make me feel fuzzy and it's making it hard to think, and I already don't do that very well.

With a jerk, I cut off the flow of love out of me and into him and the big feelings that were making thinking hard stop so quickly that I start panting like I've just run for an hour on the treadmill.

Santanos grunts and winces like it hurts, but when he opens his eyes, he's not mad or upset. He looks at me and the brightness in his core feels like it's reaching for me. "Thank you, sweetie. That was fantastic."

"Wait. Did he just feed you?" Gregory demands angrily.

"Better than an orgy of fawns," Santanos replies, but I don't know what either of those things are, so I don't get it.

Gregory though, he gets it, and he looks shocked. "You're kidding me."

Santanos smirks at him and shakes his head. "I'm not. I don't know why, but I think maybe I need to have a chat with my parents about this boy. There's something supernaturally delectable about him."

"That means you taste like his favorite food," Hassan tells me before I need to ask.

Happiness is not having to always ask my dictionary to tell me what people mean. "You're a really good evil guy, Hassan."

Hassan's love gets a little brighter again, and I know: it's because he likes me.

CHAPTER 5

Someone bangs on the door while Santanos calls to the kitchen for room service, which is so fancy, but he told me that he's rich, so I don't have to pay him back. I'm really grateful for that because I don't have any money yet. He says that he'll pay me at the end of each day so I don't have to wait two or three weeks for my first paycheck. I'm excited to be able to afford a gym membership right away.

Gregory opens the door with Hassan right behind him, so I can't see who's at the door, but then I hear my papa's digital voice. *"Let me in. I demand to see my son."*

I laugh at how insistent his computer voice sounds and get up to go to the door. "I'm here, Papa," I tell him.

Gregory makes a rude noise and Bellamy has to push Hassan out of the way, but then my papa, Bellamy, and my oppa crowd into the room.

Bellamy holds up my suitcase. "We brought clothes."

"Oh good. I was worried I would have to wear my dirty underwear," I say, relieved that I won't have to do that.

I take the suitcase to the bedroom and open it up. There's a quiet scuffle behind me, and when I look, I'm disappointed to see my family fighting with Gregory and Hassan again.

"Stop it!" I yell at them, reaching in to pull Papa off Gregory.

I hold them both at arm's length, and Bellamy gets between Oppa and Hassan.

"You can't fight with Gregory and Hassan right now; they're injured and it's not fair."

Papa stares at me with his mouth open and his eyes wide, and Oppa, who sometimes talks for him when his hands are busy, says, "We're not really worried about a fair fight, pupper."

I give him my best disappointed-grandma look. "Please stop attacking my friends, Papa. I really like Gregory and Hassan."

Papa drops his jaw to make his mouth look like a big O, but I keep my face frozen until he finally huffs and gives in, pulling away from my hand and typing. *"Fine. I won't attack your friends, but I don't trust them. They tried to kill me and Bellamy before we even met them."*

<Papa: Two words: Emotional. Manipulation.

Santanos: But we do so love the results, don't we?

Papa: I hate that I agree with you.>

I have to think about that for a second, but decide, "Well, they are evil, so that's probably ok as long as they don't actually kill you, right?"

Oppa snorts and pulls Papa under his arm, and Papa looks at him like he's not sure if Oppa agrees with me or not, but I'm pretty sure he does.

I make sure that everyone is done fighting then go back to my suitcase and grab a jock strap, dropping my towel to pull it on.

A noise behind me makes me turn to look again, and I sigh because everyone is watching me get dressed. Well, not Oppa. He's watching Papa. I don't know why they decided to watch me, but since they can't get along unless I tell them to, I think it's ok if I don't say anything about that. Instead, I just pull on a pair of shorts and a t-shirt. I tuck the shirt into my shorts and put my belt on then sit down to put my socks on.

When I turn to sit, everyone except Santanos has gone to do other things. He has a pretty smile on his face while he leans against the door, watching me. I smile back and pull my socks on, then open my arms to him because somehow I just know he wants to sit on my lap, and since I like having him close, I don't mind how much he needs to cuddle.

He walks like a fashion model toward me and sits on my lap with his arms over my shoulders. "You're fun to watch," he tells me and kisses me.

I'm not expecting a kiss, but it's nice that he likes me enough for lip kisses. "No one's ever thought I was fun. Well, my grandma used to like playing cards with me. I'm really good at card games."

Santanos' smile shines with his happiness and his laugh makes me feel fuzzy like giving him my love felt earlier, except it's a lot smaller and easier to feel. The tingles start again, but not as much, and it's nice.

"There's a group of minions who enjoy playing cards. I bet they would let you join them," he tells me. "But we're supposed to go to Milwaukee, so we'll have to wait to find out how the minions like you."

I frown at the reminder of Milwaukee. It's not a happy place right now, and I know my oppa is going to fix it because that's what he does, but, "I don't think I want to go to Milwaukee too. I've never been, and it might be ok, but I think I'd rather start working." The more days I don't work out, the more mass I lose, and I've worked really hard to get big. I don't like the idea of losing too much muscle. "Is it ok if we skip this trip?"

Santanos chuckles and nods. "Whatever you want, sweetie. I'm more than happy to skip a trip with your family. They're challenging to get along with."

I nod because he's right. "I don't know why they're so against you. You're such a nice person."

"Well, I think it might have to do with how many people I made Fox kill when I was trying to woo him to my side." He stops to think a second and shrugs. "Also, Gregory and Hassan did try to poison them, but they knew it wouldn't actually hurt them because they know how our wards work."

"I learned all about that," I tell him so he knows he doesn't have to explain that to me.

Another knock stops him from saying the next thing, and when Gregory answers the door, he calls out, "Room service is here."

"Did you get enough for my dads and brother?" I whisper, wondering if we're going to have to share and if we're all going to be a little hungry because there's not enough.

"I ordered extra," he assures me and stands up. He holds out his hand to me, so I stand up and take it, following him out to the breakfast table.

Oh good. It looks like Santanos ordered enough for everyone. The entire table is covered with plates of food. Eggs and meat and pancakes and something that looks like an egg burrito with frosting inside it. The strawberries and blueberries on the plate make me think it's probably yogurt inside the egg wrap, but I don't know what it is, so it could be anything.

Santanos hands me a fork and a plate of scrambled eggs with ham and hashbrowns. "Eat on the couch. You can come back for more."

My heart fills with love for him, and I want to kiss him again, so I bend down and peck his lips and push just a little bit of love into him again.

Santanos gasps and his eyes roll back as a smile makes his face even prettier than it always is. "You're welcome, sweetie," he whispers.

Proud of myself and happy that he knows I was saying thank you without words, I take my plate to the couch and dig in. I didn't really realize how hungry I was until now, but my stomach is pretty empty and the eggs are just like Grandma used to make. The cooks must've put some cream in them before they scrambled them up.

AFTER BREAKFAST, Santanos sits on my lap again, but this time he faces my family. "Edovard has decided to work for my organization, and since he's decided to save Gregory and Hassan from me, I've offered him the position of first assistant. He decided he would rather start working right away than go to Milwaukee with you three, and I decided to accommodate my newest employee. We've already negotiated terms. Working for me will not interfere with his Augur duties."

Since I trust Santanos not to tell them something that's not true, I listen, but my attention is on his butt because he said it's the most perfect butt in the world. I'm trying to decide if it's the way he was born or if it's something that other people can get by working out.

"He is not moving in with you," Bellamy and Oppa say at the same time, and then Papa's digital voice repeats the same words.

"Of course not. We haven't discussed living arrangements, but you were correct yesterday when you mentioned that my bedroom is not the best place for him."

I look around his back to ask, "What's wrong with your bedroom?"

Santanos glances at me, but it's Bellamy who answers. "He had it painted with scenes from a horror-porn, and we all agree that it would give you nightmares."

"Oh. Yeah. I don't watch scary movies. Well, I don't really watch movies or TV except for some cartoons when I was a kid," I tell Santanos, because my family knows I don't watch things very much.

Gregory gives me a confused look. "What do you do for fun?"

I open my mouth to answer, but Bellamy cuts me off. "Edovard's made friends with the little old ladies who live across the street from Fox and he spends time over there playing canasta."

Gregory and Hassan both give me weird looks, but it's true.

"I like them. They told me that back when they were young they weren't allowed to get married, so Franny adopted Laura so they could be family. It made me sad that they couldn't get married when they were young, but they're happy and fun to hang out with."

"I thought they were sisters," Oppa murmurs.

I shake my head and smile because I know something he doesn't. "Nope, they call each other wife even though the government thinks they're mother and daughter. I thought they could get married if they just told the government they weren't really related, but they said they didn't want to bother."

Papa's phone says, *"Those two are sweet, but getting back to the whole Edovard working for Santanos. What are his duties going to be exactly, and will you have him home for supper every night, and when are his days off, and what time does he start working? What are the benefits, the pay rate, do you offer medical? Dental?"*

Santanos leans forward, resting his elbows on his knees and showing off his perfect butt. I think maybe I could probably get a butt like that too, but I think he must do a lot of squats because it looks like a heart and mine looks long but not round like that.

"I take care of my people." He says that like it's a challenge.

"That sounds a lot like you off them when they get to be burdensome," Papa's phone says.

"Sometimes that's true," Santanos laughs, leaning back again and resting against me. "And sometimes it means that Edovard will lack for nothing while working for me, including healthcare."

"Oh, I have insurance already. My grandma's will was set up so that no matter what I will always have insurance so that if anything happens I can see a doctor or go to the emergency room," I tell them. "She didn't have much when she passed, but she made sure that I never had to worry about paying for insurance."

Everyone looks at me, including Santanos, who turns on my lap. "Your grandma set up an insurance fund for you?" he asks, like he can't believe how smart she was.

I like how she's still taking care of me even though she's been dead for a while. "Yeah. My sister got all of her other stuff, but she made sure I would always have insurance. I wish my sister would have let me have grandma's cushions that she made for me, but they were in the house when Grandma died, and I wasn't allowed to go in after that." I sigh because thinking about my sister makes me sad. "It doesn't matter. I want to be Santanos' assistant because he needs a lot of help, and I can give him what he needs. Plus Gregory and Hassan can't help him until they recover, so Santanos really needs me. And I want to meet his minions. He said we could play cards together."

Papa looks like he ate the lemon that comes in water, and Oppa pulls him into his lap, and then Bellamy groans and says, "Ok, you can work for Santanos, but you have to be home for supper every night and you are not allowed to work on Sundays no matter what and you have to have at least every other Saturday off. And you have to be happy with your job. If you start coming home upset by work and it affects your quality of life, you are not going to keep that job, because you don't need it. You can have it if you want it, but you shouldn't take it if you think you *need* it."

"Well, I need it so I can join a gym," I explain. "I can't use the home gym for gains because I've already passed the weights we have at home."

"We can buy new weights," Papa interjects.

"That's way too expensive for me right now. Plus, I like going to the gym. It's nice to workout with people who're doing the same thing. I can get tips from others and they can get tips from me. Bodybuilders can be very friendly, you know." There are a lot of reasons to join a gym like the one I was part of back in Fresno.

"I didn't know that," Papa's phone says while he looks at me surprised.

"A lot of people expect us to be mean, but my grandma told me that people who exercise have a lot of happiness in them because exercise makes people happy. It's true. People can come into the gym with dim hearts and after exercising for a little while, their hearts brighten right up." That's another good reason to go to the gym.

I turn to Hassan and Gregory to make sure they know, "Working out will help your hearts."

Gregory scowls at me. "I'm not joining a gym."

Hassan reaches over and smacks his butt. "Do we need to pat out the grumpies again?" he asks.

Gregory scowls even harder at him. "Do not."

I move Santanos to one leg and open my other arm up for Gregory, patting my lap to invite him over. "You need cuddles again," I tell him because his insides dimmed again.

With a huff, Gregory joins Santanos on my lap and I hug him close, patting his butt. Maybe he doesn't want Hassan to pat out the grumpies, but he's ok with me doing it, and as his core brightens again, mine does too. I really like Santanos' family.

"Oh my god. You can't have pets!" Papa's digital voice exclaims.

I frown at him. "You said it was ok to have Delilah in my room."

Delilah is my fish (I accidentally named a boy fish a girl name, but everyone says it's ok because the fish is as pretty as its name).

Oppa interrupts whatever Papa is about to type by putting his hand over Papa's screen. "Delilah is fine, pupper. Papa's just being dramatic. Are you coming home with us today?"

Oh, that's a good question.

I look at Santanos, who presses a kiss to my lips. "As much as I would love to monopolize you today, you should go home with your family. I'll send a car for you tomorrow."

"Ok. If you need to eat before then, you can come over or send me a message or something. Don't eat Gregory or Hassan." I make my voice sound like my grandma's when she was serious.

Santanos kisses me again, and the tingles tickle me, but it was me giving him my love again. "I promise if I need to eat, I'll come find you."

I nod and then give Gregory my attention, patting his butt to make sure he's better—he is. "Maybe Gregory should come with me," I say, doubting whether he's going to keep recovering without me.

"What a delightful idea!" Santanos exclaims at the same time Bellamy yells, "No!"

I frown at my new brother and squeeze Gregory tighter. "He's *injured*," I whisper. "He needs my help."

Papa throws his hands up, and Bellamy groans, and Oppa sighs. "The wards will only let him in the house as long as he isn't going to try to hurt anyone."

I nod and pat Gregory's butt harder. "You're going to have to pretend you're not evil while you're in my house, but we'll all know it's just pretend, and when you leave you can stop pretending."

Gregory shoots Santanos a dirty look, but then he presses his face into my neck. "Fine," he agrees.

I let out a relieved breath and rub his butt so he knows he's making the right choice. "I'm very proud of you Gregory. Doing hard things even when we don't want to is something we can be proud of." That's what my grandma used to say, and it must be true because even though he groans like he disagrees, Gregory's love gets a little brighter.

"I can't wait for tomorrow," Santanos giggles.

Hassan grunts and his core gets a little brighter too.

I'm excited about tomorrow too.

CHAPTER 6

I jerk out of a dead sleep, shooting up as the image of another scary man appears in my mind. "Rodney Calvin Gracin. Naperville, Illinois. He's selling really bad drugs that are killing people."

I take a ragged breath, and remember what Oppa told me to do when I get messages from the magic about who needs Oppa to kill them. I turn on the camera and repeat what I just said in a video and send it to the depot, who will set up the contract for Rodney's murder.

I can't believe I'm the person the universe decided to help it murder people, but Oppa explained that some people do things that are so bad they tip the balance of good and evil, and those people have to die so that the balance can be restored. I'm not super smart, but I understand that. Even though Santanos is evil, he would never do anything so evil that it hurt the entire planet.

"Are you done?" Gregory croaks from beside me.

I set my phone back on my nightstand and lay back down next to him, spooning him from behind. "I'm sorry for waking you up."

"Not your fault, pupper," he grunts, snuggling in and holding my arm close to his chest.

I smile into his hair and kiss his head. He's getting better, and feeding him my love is helping a lot. He wasn't even grumpy with me for waking him up.

He falls back to sleep first, but I'm quick to follow him, and the next time I wake up, it's because my phone is playing my wake-up song. I turn off my alarm and start my morning playlist, putting my phone above my head so I can listen to the first couple of songs before getting up.

Gregory grunts unhappily, but his love core looks so much better after just one night with me, so I'm not too worried about the grumpy guts. I make sure he's tucked into me nice and tight and kiss his head. "We'll get up in a couple of songs," I tell him so he knows he doesn't have to jump out of bed yet.

"You're the weirdest person I know," he grumps, but he's clinging to my arm like he's been doing all night, and that proves he likes me even though he thinks I'm weird.

"You're the grumpiest person I know, but I like you just the way you are."

He grunts again, but that means he likes me too. I can tell by the way his love lights up just like Hassan's did yesterday.

After a couple of songs, my get-up song starts playing—"Happy" by Will Pharrell—so I roll away from Gregory and smack his bottom. "That's the get up song; come on."

Gregory groans, but he sits up too, looking grumpy and sleepy. He scowls at me but I smile, stretching up and down. I let the music move me, wiggling with the beat. Gregory's jaw drops and his face forms a horrified expression, but I know he's exaggerating, because when I offer him my hand while dancing his love brightens just the teeniest bit. Being around me is really good for him. It's going to take a few weeks, but eventually he's going to be back to full health, and then he'll be able to feed Santanos again.

"Come on, Gregory, wiggle with me. It's the funnest," I invite him, giving him the puppy-dog look my grandpa used to give my grandma to get her to do something she didn't want to. It usually worked, and it always made her love grow happy.

Gregory reacts just like Grandma used to and lets me pull him to his feet, grumbling about dancing with me, but his hips wiggle and his insides get brighter and it's the perfect way to start a good morning.

After we dance, Gregory takes a shower, and then I do, and when we're both dressed, we go downstairs to the kitchen where Papa left two plates for breakfast and a note that Gregory reads to me.

"Dear my beloved pupper and the bastard that spent the night with him, Fox, Bellamy, and I left early for Milwaukee. We have a stop close to Chicago on our way home, but we should be back tomorrow or the next day unless there's more work in that region to be done. Take care of yourself and remember that you have to be home for supper every night. The Grandpas are bringing dinner tonight. Love, Papa."

I take the note from Gregory and crumple it up. "I'll talk to him about being nicer with his words. I can't make him like you, but I can ask him to be nicer to you," I promise, pretty sure I can get Papa to stop using mean words about my friends.

Gregory snorts. "I don't care."

I frown, handing him one of the plates Papa left us. "I care, Gregory. If he respects me, he should respect my friends." At least that's what my Grandpa told me.

Gregory pulls the aluminum foil off his plate, revealing Papa's best pancakes. He puts oatmeal and blueberries in them and crumbled up bacon. They're really filling and taste good with the blueberry syrup that Oppa makes from the harvest off his blueberry bush in the garden.

I quickly uncover my plate and then grab the syrup from the microwave, which I knew Papa would leave in there for me because he told me that he would do that if he ever has to leave before I get to eat.

"Try this; it's so good. My oppa makes it from scratch. He even grows his own blueberries," I explain, pouring syrup onto Gregory's pancakes.

I add some to mine and then realize we don't have forks, so I grab a couple from the drawer and sit down, cutting a bite of pancake and shoving it into my face. It's so good. Papa is probably a better cook than my grandpa, who was pretty decent, though neither of them are as good as my grandma. She was amazing, which is why it was always so sad that we ran out of food before I'd gotten enough.

Gregory eats without distracting me from my food, and when we're done, I clean up. After I'm done, Gregory tells me that our ride is outside, so we leave the house, taking a cab to our jobs.

"Remember that you're not supposed to feed Santanos until your core is healed," I remind him after the cab drops us off in front of a skyscraper that's surrounded by other skyscrapers. "Wow." Looking up at all the tall buildings makes me feel short, and I can't remember ever feeling short before. That's kind of fun.

"You look like a tourist," Gregory grumps, pulling me toward the glass doors that lead into the building.

The inside of the building is a long corridor with glass front businesses on each side and a bank of elevators at the center of the businesses. The corridor is split into two walkways with potted plants and couches and chairs. There's a sign with a directory for each floor, but that's not really helpful for me unless I want to stand there studying it for a while. Fortunately, Gregory knows where we're supposed to go because he heads straight for the elevators, and when we get on one—it's pretty crowded with all sorts of people—he tells the person pushing buttons to take us to the fiftieth floor.

There are a lot of stops along the way, and when we eventually get to our stop, we're the last ones on the elevator except for a reptile woman who ignores us and walks ahead of us. I'm a little surprised that she doesn't talk to us because she's full of light, but I guess maybe she's shy.

Gregory takes us straight to an office with a big sign on it and a symbol on it that kind of looks like an arrow pointing down with a goatee. He walks in, holding the door as I pass and shutting it behind me.

Hassan is lounging on the couch, reading something on his phone, and Santanos is sitting at his desk, looking so pretty with his curly blond hair looking like an angel's halo around his head. He's reading while a couple of women sit on the couch opposite Hassan, kissing like they're trying to eat each other's mouths. They're feeding Santanos, but he looks up from his reading when we enter the room, and he brightens when he sees me, jumping up and over his desk with a wide smile, launching himself into my arms.

Thankfully I catch him, and all the good feelings that always bubble up inside me when I'm with him make their appearance. I hug him close, taking a deep breath so I can smell that burning sage scent he puts off. "I really like the way you smell," I mumble into the skin on his neck.

Santanos clings to me, and I hear him sniff me too. "I like the way you smell. Like shea oil and the rivers of lava that flow through Hell."

"I use shea oil to keep my skin from getting ashy," I explain, but I don't have an explanation for why I smell like lava.

Santanos pulls back and presses a kiss to my lips, which makes all the tingles inside me explode all at once. I've never felt anything like it, and I don't understand it, but I like it, so I kiss him too, and it's just as good as when he kisses me.

His tongue licks my lips, which makes my heart start beating faster, and since I've seen kissing with tongues before, I try that. I open my mouth a little, and Santanos' tongue slides inside and touches mine.

Oh wow. That's—is there a word for something that makes you feel like you're about to fall over, but it's a good feeling? It's a good thing I'm strong, because my knees feel a little squishy and my heart wants to just gallop right on out of my chest, and for some reason it feels like Santanos isn't close enough. It's like he needs to be inside me, and when he moans it's like I'm tasting his voice. It's the best thing I've ever felt.

I tighten my arms around him, and that distracts me from our kiss long enough to realize that I started pushing my love into him again. It's ok, though, because I like feeding him, even though yesterday I got a little scared. Today I'm expecting the tingles to get really intense, so it's ok when my penis starts to act strange, though I do pull away from his kiss when we get to that point.

He breathes heavily, but the expression on his face is a good one. He looks like he just ate the best cheesecake in the world and has some leftovers for later. It's always nice when you know you can have more of your favorite later. Leftovers are the best, right? It means that you got enough to eat *and* you can have more later.

"You are dismissed," Santanos murmurs, lazily waving at the women who were kissing on the couch.

As they leave, I put Santanos down, examining his core to make sure he's getting enough to eat. Those women's cores were pretty dim, but I could tell it wasn't because of Santanos' needs. He was barely taking anything from them when we walked in.

He looks healthy and full, so that's good. I turn to check out Hassan, who looks up from his reading when I do, staring at me with his blank face. His core looks about the same as yesterday, which I don't like. He should be recovering if Santanos isn't stealing his love.

I reach out with my hand, inviting him in for a hug.

He doesn't react on the outside, except to get up and walk to me, but his core brightens just a tiny bit because he likes that I care about him. I wrap my arms around him and hug him tight, letting my love feed into him. It doesn't feel like it does with Santanos because Hassan can't pull it into himself. He just has to soak it up like Gregory does.

"How long are you going to hug him?" Gregory grumps, so I reach over and pull him into my arms too, making it a three person hug.

"As long as it takes," I tell him. "It's good for him, just like cuddling is good for you."

The flash of a camera draws our attention to Santanos leaning against his desk with his phone in hand. He snaps another picture with a wicked smile. "This is going straight to the insta. The minions are going to die."

"Nooo," Gregory complains, but he doesn't try to leave the hug.

Hassan grunts and squeezes me a little tighter. "They might literally die if a single one makes fun of us."

Santanos cackles like Hassan just told the funniest joke, but I'm pretty sure he was serious.

"Maybe put a warning on the picture just so everyone knows they need to be nice in their comments." I kiss Hassan's cheek to make sure he knows that I understand that he doesn't want anyone to make fun of him for needing hugs. "I have a lot of followers on Instagram, and sometimes people don't realize how much they need someone to love them and they say mean things to people who have love in their lives. We should make sure the minions know they can't be mean because they're jealous of us."

"Who said anything about love?" Gregory demands, pulling back from my hug with a worried look on his face.

I pat his head, but let him go—it's not ok to force people to hug who don't want hugs. "Gregory, it's ok to let people love you. Santanos loves you a lot, Hassan loves you too, and so do I. I know it's hard for you to love because your core is hurting so much, but don't worry. Just let us all love you, and pretty soon your core is going to be bright and happy too. You can still be evil; I don't want you to worry about that." I add that last part because I just know Gregory would be really upset if he had to stop being evil because we fixed his love core.

Gregory's eyes get as wide as dinner plates and he backs up again. "Wha—we—you can't just—"

Hassan grumbles, steps out of my hug, and grabs Gregory. "Shut up, idiot," he says, then kisses Gregory just like Santanos kissed me.

Both of their cores light up to an almost normal brightness. The kind of brightness that most people have. It doesn't last, and when they stop kissing, their love dims again, but it takes longer than usual to lose its shine.

Santanos takes my hand. "What put that smile on your face?" he asks curiously.

"I just like how much they love each other," I shrug.

Santanos' smile makes my stomach feel a little fluttery, like I'm almost hungry and if I wait a little longer I'll work up a big appetite.

"I don't think they've ever admitted how they feel for each other," he giggles, but it makes me sad.

"You have to say it. You have to. You need to make sure the people you love hear you say it as much as you do things to show them you love them. You can't hear actions, and sometimes we do things that we think show our friends and family that we love them, but they don't understand that's what we're doing. Hassan, you have to tell Gregory you love him. You too Gregory, you have to tell Hassan."

The guys look at me like I'm talking nonsense, but I know I'm right.

"Tell each other that you love each other. It's important."

Gregory jerks like someone hit him when he and Hassan both look at each other at the same time.

Hassan takes his turn first, which is good because I don't think Gregory would do it if Hassan didn't start. "I love you. I have for decades."

Decades? That's—I grab my phone as Gregory's face looks like he just ate a lemon.

"I love you too. Probably since before you."

"What's decades?" I whisper to my phone.

I stare at the answer, which is the number ten—I can read numbers —and then I sound out the next words. It's ten years. So they've loved each other for more than one set of ten years and they haven't told each other until just now.

"And people say I'm dumb," I say aloud even though I don't mean to.

My cheeks burn with shame that I let my inside thoughts out. "Sorry! You really should have told each other that you love each other before now, but I shouldn't have said that!"

They stare at me for a blink and then Gregory laughs, and Santanos giggles, and Hassan looks less serious, and everyone's core gets a little brighter for a moment, so I guess it's ok this time.

"I'm going to give Edovard a tour," Hassan decides when Gregory and Santanos stop laughing.

Santanos pulls me down and gives me another one of those tongue kisses that feel so good. I don't have to pull away this time; instead he keeps it short and pinches my butt, which makes me smile. I like that he makes sure I know that he likes me.

"Have fun, and make sure the minions know that you're my assistant. That means that if you tell them to do something they have to do it. So don't tell them to be good, ok?" Santanos says.

"I understand. Everyone wants to be evil, so I have to make sure they're doing evil things, but it's ok if I make sure their love is healthy, right?"

Santanos' smile is so pretty and the love inside him just shines so bright in response to my words. I really love him, and it would be so hypocritical of me to not say that now that I realize it.

"I love you," I tell him, pulling him into a tight hug. "I can see why your minions love you so much." He's just like Gru from *Despicable Me*. Evil, but good.

"Awww, sweetie, I love you too," Santanos tells me, squishing me back. "And yes, you can make sure all the minions are healthy. I bet if you do that it'll be easier to bring this world back into the balance."

I pull back, remembering how Papa and Oppa explained the balance. "It's not balanced?"

"No, it's off by a couple of percentage points. If the maximum of good and evil the earth can handle in one go is a hundred kilograms, then we want the normal amount of good to be ninety kilograms and the normal amount of evil to be ten kilograms, just ten percent of the maximum the earth can handle. Right now we're at twelve percent. Twelve kilograms of evil, and we need to get back down to ten kilograms, because we want good to be at ninety kilograms all the time."

He's using percentage training to explain, and I totally understand. He's so smart, helping me to get it through things I already know. "Ok, so we want everyone to be two kilograms less evil. How will we know if it works?"

"We have a whole department that monitors that kind of thing," he promises.

I nod, feeling good about my new job. I can definitely help bring the percentages into balance. "I'll do my part," I promise.

Santanos pulls me down to kiss my cheek, and then Hassan and I leave for the tour.

CHAPTER 7

The first place Hassan takes me is down to the seventh floor where the gym is. I've known he likes me since yesterday, but this is like a gift I didn't know was coming, and I get a little excited by it, pulling him into a bear hug and kissing him before I remember I should ask permission.

"Oh sorry," I whisper because now a bunch of the gym members are staring at us. "I should have asked permission before I did that, but I got so excited. Thank you, Hassan."

He narrows his eyes and his lips turn down, but his core brightens up, so I'm glad for that, even if I made a mistake. He stares at me long enough to make me nervous; I don't want him to take away his gift, but then he shakes his head. "It's ok to kiss me and Gregory as long as Santanos doesn't mind."

A breath I didn't realize I was holding whooshes out of me, and I open my arms, asking for a forgiveness hug. Hassan huffs and gives me a quick hug and another kiss.

When he steps back, he takes me to the registration desk and gets me set up with an employee membership (it's free!). As soon as I finish with all the paperwork—Hassan helps me with reading it, but I fill it out myself—he takes me into the gym and shows me where all the equipment is and the schedule of classes.

"Do you teach pole dancing?" I whisper, pointing at a class where the instructor's name is Hassan Su.

"Yes," he confirms. "Do you want to join the class today?"

It's happening in a few minutes, but I don't have any workout clothes with me. I wipe my hand on my dress shirt and give him puppy eyes because I don't think it's rude to ask if he has any clothes I can borrow, but I can't remember if my grandma had a rule for this and I don't want to accidentally be rude.

One of Hassan's eyebrows rises curiously, so I intensify my puppy eyes and pull at my collar.

He glances down to my neck and his eyebrow drops. "Do you need workout clothes?"

I make a weird happy noise that he figured it out. "I do!"

Hassan's usually serious expression softens and his love brightens up again, and then it just stays that bright instead of slowly dimming again. "Gregory's right, you are a pupper."

I laugh and nod. "Papa tells me that too. I've decided to just accept it."

He looks like he might laugh, but he's not like that, so he just says, "Come on, you can borrow some of my shorts, but my shirts would strangle you, so you'll have to go shirtless." He turns on his heels, saying to no one in particular, "Not that anyone is going to complain."

Happy that I'm going to finally get to workout again, I follow him to the locker room where he hands me a pair of shorts from a stack of clean ones in his locker. I strip out of my button up shirt and pants and carefully fold them up, putting them in an empty locker.

"I'm glad I wore my trainers today," I tell him as I pull his shorts on.

Hassan examines me, probably to make sure I'm not going to rip his shorts. "Hmm," he grunts, as he takes his phone out. "I think Santanos would appreciate a picture."

I raise my arms in a strong man pose and smile for the camera.

He snaps a photo and tells me to give him my back, then we do a couple of profile photos. I ask him to send them to me so I can post them on my insta too, and then he changes into his workout clothes and takes me to the classroom he uses for his pole dancing class.

The other people taking the class trickle in as Hassan gets everything ready. It's pretty cool how different everyone is. There's a couple of lizard people and a person with long pointy ears, plus a bunch of normal humans. There's one person whose core is completely black, and when he looks at me, he makes me feel like he would probably kill me and my entire family for fun.

<Bellamy: We would never let anyone get that close.
Oppa: I'd let them get close enough to introduce them to my swords.
Bellamy: We wouldn't let them kill us, Pupper.>

As soon as I see the evil guy, his name pops out of my mouth. "Chance Dorian Willis." I gasp as the knowledge of what he's done wants to get out of me, but I know I can't just blurt that kind of thing in a public place like this.

Chance looks surprised and then grins. "You know me? Aren't you Santanos' new boy toy? That's cool."

I look to Hassan, who points to the door. "Go on, Edovard. Come back when you're done."

I jog out of the room, anxious to get to my phone. I grab it out of my locker and go find an empty classroom, where I make my video and send it to the depot. That guy is bad enough to get on Oppa's list, and now that I've seen his black core, I understand what Oppa and Papa were trying to tell me. The world really would be better off without people like Chance. He's that kind of evil.

As soon as my message to the depot goes through, I pocket my phone, but I decide not to go back to the class because I don't think it would be good for me to be in the same room as the guy the universe wants my oppa to kill. That's just awkward. So I just find a treadmill and warm up on it.

The person next to me is a happy minion with plenty of pretty blue love inside her. She's running on the machine in a sports tank and leggings, and her blond hair is swinging side to side in the ponytail she put it in. She reminds me of how movies portray sorority girls. I always thought they were probably exaggerating how mean the sorority sisters were, and based on her core, I think I was probably right about that.

"You're doing good," I tell her as I jog beside her.

"Thanks?" She says that like she's confused.

"The machine says you've been running for twenty minutes already and you've done three miles. You're doing good, and sometimes we need other people to recognize our accomplishments. I'm just recognizing yours. Good job." I give her an encouraging smile. "I always do better when someone else tells me I'm doing well too."

Her smile looks more real when she understands why I'm talking to her, and her core twinkles with happiness. "Thank you. You're right; it's nice to hear, isn't it."

I point to my phone, which I put in the cupholder so I wouldn't get it sweaty through my shorts. "That's why I have an insta. I have a bunch of followers that help me see I'm doing good. They're very encouraging."

She grimaces at my phone. "I tried that, but I just got a bunch of messages from disgusting men trying to get me naked."

That makes me sad, but I get it. "Yeah, I get those too. I don't know why guys do that. Some women too, but not too many. You don't have to do it like me; I'll come in every day to tell you you're doing good, and that way you know someone is cheering for you."

Her smile reappears and she laughs, shaking her head at me. "Sure, buddy. What's your name?"

"Oh, right." I should have introduced myself first. "I'm Edovard Folange. I'm Santanos' new assistant. What's your name?"

"Erica Montrose. I'm the accountant in charge of the tax evasion team."

"What's that?" I ask curiously.

"I just find ways of cheating the government out of the taxes the company would owe if the IRS knew how much money we actually rake in."

Oh! I know what that is! There was a big news story about this that my grandpa explained to me once. "Oh, that's bad. Good job! I heard about the guy who had a charity set up that only donated stuff to his friends so they could get stuff like new phones and cars—I don't know how that stuff works for taxes, but I bet you're smarter than that guy's accountants since they got caught."

She laughs again and nods. "I think we're smarter for sure. We don't have any false charities."

"When I was a kid, there was a community center that I went to all the time because they had a gym I was allowed to use. I think that kind of charity would be cool for us to have. We could have a safe space for kids and teens that need a place, and I think that's also a good way to avoid paying taxes, right?" Maybe that's too noble for the minions of evil.

She gives me a thoughtful look and nods slowly. "Yeah, that might be a good way to recruit new minions too. If their parents aren't going to raise them, then they can't blame us for instilling questionable morals."

I don't know about that. Something about that sounds wrong, but not like the kind of wrong that's ok. "I don't think we should teach them to be evil. At least, not behind their parents' backs, right?"

"No, you're right. We won't teach them about good and evil, we'll just give them life skills that might lean toward less savory job choices. We can teach lockpicking, sneaking, tetris—ooh, I bet chemistry would be important if they wanted to become chemists and math because we don't want anyone cheating them out of their cut of the profits. Business classes and marketing strategies in case they decide to be small business owners or open laundromats. This is a fantastic idea. I'm going to see if we can recruit some minions to make this happen. Children are totally the future." She laughs and jumps off her treadmill, punching my arm happily. "See you tomorrow, Edovard!"

Happiness makes me go extra hard on the treadmill after she leaves. Even if the minions are evil, at least they're going to be helping kids, which is good. Maybe we can be evil and also so full of love for the world that we make it a world worth being evil in. Hmmm, I wonder if they're like the supervillains and they want to take over the world, but more like Megamind and just want to have fun trying to take over the world but not actually succeeding because that would tip the percentages in the wrong direction.

That's a question to ask Santanos. I think we should have goals. We have to be able to see our gains or we're going to get discouraged and maybe fall off the wagon, and then we'll all be unhappy. It's like exercise; maybe we have a lifetime goal, and maybe that's not always something we get to see happen, but our one month goal and our one year goal should be things we can definitely accomplish.

Since I'm feeling good and warm and my heart rate is up, I step off the treadmill and jog over to the free weights, deciding to go a little easy on myself since I haven't worked out in a while. Today I'll just remind my muscles that they can lift plenty of weight. I can do lesser weights and higher reps and that will help remind my body that it loves to work hard.

I plan to work all my muscle groups, and then tomorrow I'll start my regular lifting schedule again. I just have to go over my journal and make a plan to get back to where I was before I moved in with my new family. I'll do that before bed tonight, but for now, I'm going to enjoy having a gym again.

CHAPTER 8

After a really good workout and a shower to clean off the sweat, Hassan finishes the tour of the building, taking me to each floor and introducing me around. I get to meet a lot of people, and by the time we get to the accounting floor, Erica has news about the youth center idea—I almost didn't recognize her because she changed into a tight red dress with a big black belt and heels that make her almost as tall as Hassan.

"You look really nice in your dress," I compliment her so she knows that I'll cheer her on even outside of the gym.

She gives me a nice smile and pats my arm. "Thank you, Edovard. Let me tell you about what the acquisitions department said when I asked about properties that we might be able to use for a youth center…"

She tells me about a neighborhood that needs support and a building that they can use, but I don't really understand all the big words and details that she uses. Fortunately Hassan is listening, and I'm sure he can explain it to me later.

I'm not ashamed of myself because I'm not as smart as Erica, but I don't want to use up her time explaining everything twice. She seems excited, and I know that when I'm excited I can get a lot done. I don't want to stand in the way of her excitement.

After we say goodbye to her, Hassan and I get in the elevator again and he hits the button for the top floor before turning back to me. "We're going to have lunch with Santanos before we hit the upper floors."

A fluttery feeling starts in my stomach at the mention of Santanos. It's funny, but I think he's one of my favorite people on the planet even though I only met him a few weeks ago. I know that he's supposed to be part of my life; he's always been so nice to me and his love shines so brightly that I just want to be around him all the time.

"I really do love him," I blurt out. I can't keep that love to myself, even if Santanos isn't here to hear me.

Hassan's expression doesn't change, but the light of his love flares really bright for a second. He appreciates that I love Santanos, and I like that.

"He's easy to love," Hassan says and steps closer to me.

I smile and close the distance between us, offering him a hug and getting a fake annoyed sigh and a hug. Hassan likes to pretend he doesn't want my hugs, but he's a liar, and that's ok because he's evil and also because I can see the truth inside him. I kiss his forehead, and he turns his face toward mine, kissing my lips but not like Santanos kisses me.

Just before the elevator stop, Hassan pulls back, stepping out of my hug, but he holds my hand, which is nice. I really like how important touching is to the evil side too. It makes me happy how many people want to hug and hold hands and give me kisses. It's like I finally found the right place for me.

We step into Santanos' office and Hassan closes the door behind us. Santanos is on the phone, pacing the open office space, and Gregory is using Santanos' desk to work on a stack of paperwork. He looks cute when he looks up over a pair of rectangle glasses sitting on the end of his nose. He notices that Hassan is holding my hand and his inner love pulses a little brighter.

Even though these two never told each other they love each other before, they're so happy when the other is happy. They're really good partners for each other, and it makes my heart happy seeing how much they care about each other. They're just like my grandparents were: full of happiness for and with each other, but they share that happiness with me too, so it's even better.

"I'm looking at his work schedule right in front of me. Chance will be at the call center at nine PM tomorrow night and the night after, but then he's off until Monday." Santanos is lying to whoever's on the phone because he's not looking at anything.

He snorts and rolls his eyes. "We're on the same team," he says into the phone, and then his wickedness makes him grin at me. "Hey, baby boy. How was the tour?" He laughs without waiting for an answer. "Yes, Edovard is standing in my office holding my bodyguard's hand."

"I'll let you talk to him if you admit we're on the same team."

He laughs and his love lights up with his happiness, and then he hands me his phone. "It's your Grand Sugar Daddy."

I put the phone to my ear. "Granddaddy?"

Papa's sugar daddy is Annette, the Avatar of Good, which is Santanos' opposite. She's fun and nice, and she bought me some really nice gifts and a watch that will keep track of my workouts once I figure out how to set that up. *"Pupper! Are you ok? Blink twice if you're in danger and need Grandaddy to come rescue you from the minions of evil."*

I blink and then accidentally blink again. "No! I didn't mean to blink! Grandaddy, I'm ok. I like it here. I got to start a youth center for kids who need extra support today. It's going to be great! We're going to teach business classes and teach them how to do laundry and how to count money. Erica said we're going to make sure the kids have a lot of life skills. Sometimes I wish someone had taught me life skills like that. Oh." I turn to Hassan to tell him what I just thought of. "We should have a reading class because some kids have a hard time reading and it would be nice if we can help them."

My grand sugar daddy makes a nice noise and coos, "Aww pupper, I'm so proud of you! You've already started a charity!"

"Yes. I was helping the tax e-something person figure out a way to make sure the government doesn't get money."

"Tax evasion?" she asks.

"Yes. That. Evasion."

"It's a great idea," she says, but she's lost some of her excitement. "Since you're ok, I'm going to hang up, but I hope to see you tonight. The grandfathers are going to treat you like a little prince tonight, and I want to be there."

I smile. "Ok, Grandaddy. I can't wait to see you." It's so nice to have grandparents again. "Love you."

"Love you too, sweet thing."

She hangs up and I give Santanos back his phone. "She's the best."

"She's literally the Avatar of Good, so I would expect so," Santanos laughs, pulling me down for another one of those exciting tongue kisses. French kissing. Hassan mentioned it earlier when he told some minions that if they're going to French kiss they needed to do it closer to Santanos' floor because they were too far away for Santanos to get anything from it.

That feeling that he's too far away comes back, and I wrap him up in my arms and pull him against me. I know he likes it when I carry him, so I don't ask.

The tingles start as soon as he wraps his legs around my waist and gather in my lower half again, but I push the boundaries of my comfort zone instead of stopping when it gets weird. I like kissing Santanos, and I know he's going to stop when I need to, but we both want me to be able to kiss longer, so I push my comfort a little and stop whenever it feels like my underwear is too small.

That's too weird a feeling for me to enjoy kissing anymore. I take a deep breath and calm down, slowing the trickle of love that I keep pushing into Santanos. He licks my neck and sniffs me, which is a little weird but doesn't hurt me, so he can lick me if he wants. I let him lick my tongue; it might be weird if I said something about him licking my neck.

"Why do you smell so good?" he groans, and this time he bites my neck.

I jump at the flash of pain and yelp, but the strange thing is that I feel it in my balls. I didn't know my neck was connected to my balls.

"I used Hassan's lotion after we showered earlier." I manage to get that out through a lump in my throat.

It feels like I'm nervous, but I'm not. Santanos is nice and easy to get along with. He keeps doing things that I'm not used to, and I just have to get used to the way he shows his love. It's ok to be uncomfortable with new people—I'll keep reminding myself of that, and I'll get used to it, and then I'm going to really appreciate all the ways they make me feel important and all the new ways I can make them feel important too.

"Have you called your father?" Hassan asks from his seat on the sofa against the wall.

Santanos shoots him a dirty look. "Why must you always remind me of things I don't want to do?"

Hassan grunts and raises his eyebrow at Santanos. "Is there anything you want to do right now other than fuck Edovard?"

"Obviously not," Santanos sniffs, looking away from Hassan with his nose in the air.

He's so cute when he's being silly. I kiss his cheek with a smile. "You can't have sex at work, and I don't even know if I want to have sex anyway. You can call your dad after lunch."

Santanos smirks at me and his light shines so bright that it feels like it warms me up from the inside. "I just ate, but I am always up for seconds, sweetie."

I know what that means, so I kiss him again, opening up my love on purpose this time to feed him as much as I can before my body gets too strange for me again.

This time when I pull back, Santanos' eyes stay closed and his face is tipped upward like he's enjoying a really delicious bite. I love that the love I feed him tastes so good to him. It makes me happy to exist, and existing hasn't always been happy for me, but I don't like to think about that.

<Papa: Pupper, sometimes you say things like that and it makes me want to let Oppa kill people. Should we get our boy into some therapy?

Bellamy: His past isn't making it difficult for him to live in the present.

Oppa: And he's good at working through his emotions.

Gregory: Edovard is the smartest of all of us about emotions, so I don't *think therapy is necessary. But you should definitely talk to us about the things that hurt you so that we can help.*

Hassan: Sharing a burden makes it easier for everyone to bear.

Me: Ok, but not right now. Maybe after I'm done talking to the computer.

Santanos: That's reasonable.>

My stomach grumbles and Santanos' eyes pop open. He smiles and unhooks his legs, jumping down to his own feet. "Come along, Edovard. Let's feed you. Hassan? Gregory? Eating here or with us?"

Gregory gives Santanos a dirty look. "I am working on your reports. If I want to sleep tonight, I can't stop every time you need a break."

Hassan stands, grabs Gregory by the arm, and yanks him to his feet. "Delegate after lunch," he insists, pulling Gregory to the door.

Gregory screeches something that isn't English—it sounds like a lot of naughty words—but Hassan doesn't stop and gets him out the door and to the elevator.

Gregory only stops yelling when Hassan pushes him into the elevator and the doors close.

"I think Gregory is going to punch Hassan," I blurt out.

Santanos giggles, taking my hand and sliding his fingers between mine. "It wouldn't be the first time."

"Even I can see that." I've seen a lot of best friends come to blows, and Gregory's anger was definitely dark enough to hit, but I think Hassan is cool enough to forgive Gregory.

"What kind of food do you want for lunch, sweetie?" Santanos asks as he leads me to the elevators too.

I give it some thought, listening to my body about what it might be craving right now. "I think I'd like chicken and rice."

We enter the elevator together and he hits the button for the ground floor. "I know a demon that makes the most delicious rice pilaf I've ever had. I prefer his tuna dish, but the chicken is just as good."

I don't know what pee-loft is, but it's probably not what it sounds like, and Santanos wouldn't feed me anything disgusting. "Do you mind ordering for me like you did before?"

He kisses the back of my hand and the flutters in my stomach make another appearance. "I don't mind ordering food for you for the rest of your life, sweetie. Do you want me to be in charge of that when we go out to eat?"

Sighing because he's the nicest man I've ever met, I pull him into a hug. "Thank you. I would really like that."

He giggles and smacks a kiss against my cheek. "You delight the hell out of me. I'll do all the ordering, but make sure you tell me if you enjoy something or if you don't. I don't want to find out that you're forcing yourself to eat something you hate."

I laugh, happy that he won't make me eat things I don't like. I've always thought it was a little mean that some people had to eat things they didn't like, but my grandma never cooked me things I wouldn't like, so I'm glad Santanos has the same rules about food that she did. "I promise I will tell you if I don't like something."

"Good boy," he says, sending a nice wave of happiness into me, so I return my happiness by letting my love trickle into him.

CHAPTER 9

"Stop," I tell Santanos, digging my heels in to stop him from following the waiter at the restaurant.

Santanos stops and turns, surprise on his face.

I look around the restaurant. Most of the wait staff are as dim inside as Gregory was the other day. Someone is killing their love, and that person is behind the door to the kitchen. All their love is being pulled right out of them and flying through the door to the back.

I let go of his hand, waving at the restaurant as a whole. "I get that we're evil and we're supposed to be evil, but why are we giving up our happiness to do it? Look at these poor waiters! Whoever is in the kitchen is stealing their love just like you were doing with Gregory. These people deserve to be happy! They should be allowed to keep their love inside them. I'm not going to let whoever is behind that door keep taking their love." I can't help it if I'm getting angry and loud. I don't care that all the waiters stop serving and start staring at me. I don't care that some of the people eating are looking at me like I'm the bad guy. This is unacceptable!

I don't wait for Santanos to answer; I march straight to the kitchen, banging the door louder than I expected, looking for the person stealing everyone's love.

He's easy to spot. His inner self is a black hole of pure darkness, and his eyes are as black as night. I pull out my phone and start a video. "Saxon Lucy Sybil the Third. You've eaten too much love and now my Oppa is coming for you!" I announce then send the video to the depot.

The black man's face was already scowling when I marched into his kitchen, but now he looks like he wants to kill me. He screams at me and throws a black hand of magic from his core at me and grabs the love inside me.

I'm not going to just let him steal all the love inside me, especially when it's not going to help him at all. I don't know how I do it, but I just do. I use my own love to grab his darkness and then I think about how much Santanos loves me and how much my new family loves me and it makes my insides bright enough that I just snuff out the darkness, like when you turn on the lights in a scary room and it's not scary anymore.

His darkness doesn't stand a chance against my light, and when it disappears his scream goes from angry to pained. He falls on his butt, staring up at me like I'm the bad guy, but we both know it's him, not me.

"You need to leave now. I'm not going to let you keep hurting all these people," I tell him, pointing at the back door.

Saxon crawls away from me and then scrambles out of the back door, tripping in his hurry to get out, but when finally he's gone, and I look around at all the scared faces of the cooks whose love he was stealing too. "It's ok. He's not going to hurt you anymore. If you want to feel better, I can hug anyone and help you get some love back. I have a lot in my life, so I can share it."

"Did you just kick my son out of my restaurant?"

I turn around to the person asking that, finding him standing with Santanos in the doorway. "He was stealing everyone's love right out of them. He wasn't even using it like Santanos does. He was just hurting people to hurt them, and these cooks and the waiters don't deserve that kind of treatment. And the magic decided he'd done enough damage."

"Edovard is an Auger," Santanos explains.

The dark man, I guess he's Saxon's father, looks angry and huffs his annoyance. His insides are gray-ish, but like a cloudy day, not too dark. He's still got some love in him; he just needs to do more things that make him happy and find more people he can love and that will love him. "So Fox is going to kill him? Fox has killed seven of my children. I'm beginning to think I'm a terrible father."

Santanos giggles. "You're a soul-sucking demon; you *are* a terrible father. Though how you manage to create spawn that are worse than you is a mystery."

Saxon sighs and shakes his head. "It's their mother's fault. If she would stop sending our spawn to this plane, they would stop getting reaped. She only sends the one's she hates, though, so maybe she's doing it on purpose."

I frown at them. "You should love them better and maybe they would be better people."

Santanos holds his hand out to me. "Saxon's species spawns hundreds of worms at a time. They eat each other until only one remains, and then that one gets to become an adult. Their entire existence starts with being the strongest and most brutal. It's not actually surprising that they're more evil than this world can handle."

"They start out as worms?" I ask, looking at Saxon to see if he has wormy features and I didn't notice. He doesn't. He just looks like a normal person.

"Yes. Our species starts as cannibalistic worms. The spawn eat each other to build up the strength and mass to pupate into their bipedal form." He waves at his body, so I guess that means that they transform into people.

I'm kind of sad that they have to eat each other, but it's not their fault how their species works, and maybe I should just be grateful that some of them survive.

"Um. I'm sorry that you keep having your kids murdered."

He blows out a breath. "It's fine. If they're actually creating enough problems to tip the balance, then they deserve what they get."

Harsh. I don't like Saxon at all, but his people need help. "I need to hug all the waiters and cooks who want hugs to make them feel better."

Saxon waves like he doesn't care. "Go on then. Everyone who needs a hug get it now. I'll let our patrons know their lunches will be delayed."

"I'll pay for everyone's lunches," Santanos murmurs as Saxon turns to go.

Saxon bows to him and leaves me in the kitchen with the staff.

I open my arms. "If you want hugs to help you heal, I am a really good hugger and I can help your insides feel less bad. That guy was really doing a number on you."

One of the girls in a chef's coat puts her knife down and walks around the table and straight into my arms. I hug her tight and push as much love as she can take into her, rubbing her back to help her relax so she can absorb more. When everyone else sees that she's safe, two more people come and turn it into a group hug, and I push my love into them too, then the rest of them join us, and the group hug really works because they start pulling the love instead of me pushing it, and they start sharing it between them too, so everyone starts brightening up faster than I expected.

It's a relief to see them getting better so quickly, and they're good at sharing, too, because they shuffle from the front of the hug right next to me to the back, letting their friends get in close so everyone gets a good hug from me. It takes a little bit of time, but everyone gets a turn and a proper refill of their love from my core, even the waiters. They all look and feel better afterward. There are a lot more smiles on faces when everyone gets back to work.

Happy to have helped, I turn to find Santanos, but he left the kitchen at some point. I walk back out to the dining room and find him sipping on some wine while talking to Saxon at a two person table. I walk over to them and pick Santanos up, sitting in his chair with him on my lap since I know he likes to sit this way. Plus, I get to brag about having the most perfect butt in the world on my lap, and that makes me super happy even though I don't really understand why I feel that way yet. Don't worry, I'll figure it out.

Sometimes people like things and there isn't a good reason for it. If everyone is happy, and nobody's getting hurt, then it's probably ok.

I try to listen to their conversation, but it's kind of boring, so I pull out my phone and use the learning app that Papa got me to help me learn tools for reading. He thinks we just have to figure out the right tools for me to learn how to read better, and he says if this app doesn't work, we'll try something else. Since no one ever really had the time to help me read better, I'm excited to try. I know it's going to be work, but so is body building, and I do that work all the time. This is just brain building, so I'm treating it like exercise. I have short term and long term goals, and I have a timeline, and I even made a schedule so I can stay on target for my gains. Brain gains are just like muscle gains.

After I finish my lesson—it's a good one and I have a good feeling about this app—our food is brought to the table, and without interrupting his conversation, Santanos starts feeding me. He just forks up some chicken and holds it for me to bite. Since I'm holding him, and it would be awkward to try to eat around him, I'm glad he came up with a good solution. He feeds me bites and I eat, and Saxon watches, and they talk, and it's a really good lunch. Plus there's enough food for all of us.

Santanos figures out when I get full without me telling him, and I get to just cuddle him and let my love seep into him while he eats his share. I rest my forehead on his shoulder, closing my eyes and just soaking up the goodness in my life since I left Fresno.

I don't know if there's such a thing as God, but if there is, I hope they know I'm really thankful for my new life.

CHAPTER 10

Santanos waves at the taxi that is waiting for us after lunch, takes my hand, and walks past our ride. "I feel like walking. We didn't get any privacy during our lunch date, and I'd like to spend some time with you."

My heart gets happy in my chest when he says that. The only people who wanted to spend any time with me before were the gym guys that I knew, but they didn't really want to hang out after our workouts—they were always really busy—but Santanos wants to spend time with me!

"I want to spend time with you too. Plus it's nice to walk holding hands, isn't it? It's like one of those romantic movies my grandma used to like watching during the holidays. I didn't like them, but it's different when you're doing it than watching it. I like holding your hand."

For some reason, the way Santanos looks when he smiles up at me makes it hard to breathe again. The sunshine makes the blond curls shine like he's the reason sunbeams even exist, and his blue eyes look brighter and lighter than ever, and I don't know how I never noticed before, but he has dimples. I've been so focused on his insides that I completely missed dimples! He's shorter than me, but he feels so big that it's like I'm his moon.

It's amazing how fast a person can get attached to another person.

Like how Papa just decided that I belonged to him without even knowing anything about me. I guess that's how it is for me and Santanos too.

<Papa: This is not my fault.

Oppa: ...

Bellamy: It's a little bit your fault.

Santanos: You have my thanks for setting such a wonderful example of love and devotion for our pupper.>

"I like holding your hand as well, darling. I'd like to know more about you, and I'd like you to know more about me, too. Can you think of anything that you want to know?" I love how his voice sounds just like it was made for my ears to hear him. Listening to him is as nice as looking at him, and even better, he listens to me too and wants to answer my questions!

"What is your favorite food?" I blurt out, excited to get to learn all about him.

"You, my love," he teases me, "but I enjoy a little dish from my home realm called" —He makes noise that sounds fun to say— "which basically means stewed wildflower soaked in the blood of my enemy and harvested from between the bones. It's a nostalgic dish for me and reminds me of my childhood."

I have to think about that for a minute. "Just so I know, is the flower actually soaked in blood?" I whisper to make sure.

"Yes. It's a special kind of flower that can only grow on battlefields where blood is spilled," he explains.

<Papa: I'm not usually judgey...

Oppa: *inhuman noise* is delicious. It's a staple of Hellion cuisine.

Santanos: It's traditional for children to go harvest the flowers for the dish together. The activity builds strong familial bonds and healthy competition between siblings. My eldest brother started the tradition thousands of years before I was born.

Oppa: I don't think murdering your brother in an open field counts as starting a tradition...

Santanos: Potato, Potahto.>

That's kind of gross, but I don't want to be insensitive to his culture, so I shrug and kiss his hand and say, "Maybe I'll get to try it with you sometime." But I hope not too soon. Maybe if he didn't tell me what it was and I liked it and then he told me it was that stuff it would be ok.

"Maybe," he hums thoughtfully. "My turn. Tell me in detail everything that you would have taken from your grandparents house if you could have? I would also like to know your sister's name."

"Her name is Manon Folange." I don't really want to talk about her, so I talk about the things in my grandma's house that I wanted. "She made me a bunch of pillows and cushions for my nest when I was a kid. I didn't do well sleeping alone, so they were all warm and soft, but she put sand in them to make them heavy like a body. Sometimes when I was very sad, she would warm them up for me so it was like I had someone sleeping with me. I wasn't allowed to take them when she died, and it was kind of hard to learn to sleep without them. I don't really like sleeping alone, but that's what I'm supposed to do, so I learned how."

"It's a good thing that you're taking Gregory home with you tonight. It would be lonely in that house all by yourself," he says, making me feel important. I didn't really think about Gregory staying again, but it's good someone is, because he really needs to be with me.

"I'm really glad he's going to be with me."

Before I can think of another question to ask, the gargoyle friends that like to help my family out sometimes start getting really loud. They sound like church bells, but I didn't know what church bells sounded like until I heard it. It's a nice sound, even when they are all talking at the same time. I don't know their language, but Santanos looks like he does. He gives the gargoyle friends on the buildings his attention, and then his eyes get really big like he's surprised.

Suddenly, he yanks me by the arm and I go flying into the building we're walking by (he's super strong, but you can't tell because his body is so small) (and soft) (I like it). There's the sound of something hitting the sidewalk really hard, and when I turn around Santanos is fighting a huge guy with a really big hammer.

The guy is bigger than me and his skin is ashy gray and he's got tiny little black eyes. He's bald, too, and naked. There are a lot of people on the street, but they just cross the road before they get to the fight (that's weird right?), and no one seems to even notice or care about the big guy with the hammer the size of my head trying to kill Santanos.

Santanos ducks and weaves around the guy with the hammer. Thankfully he's really fast, so he doesn't get hit. I don't know if his ward will work against a hammer that big, and I get worried thinking about it. What if he gets hit? I don't want him to get hurt—

Before I can get too worked up about the fight, Santanos does something with his magic that reaches out to the heart of the guy's darkness, and it lights the guy up from the inside out. The guy freezes in his tracks, and his penis gets big, and then he starts shooting all over the sidewalk. If I was him, I'd be pretty embarrassed by that—he's supposed to be fighting, and then he's doing public sex. Even I know that's supposed to be private.

Santanos steals all the light that he just made inside the guy, and I think that's fine since he's the one that put it there, and then the guy falls on his knees. The second he's down, Santanos takes the hammer in one hand and bashes him in the head.

I'm not ashamed to say I lose my lunch on the sidewalk. Fortunately there's a bunch of gargoyles around, and they swarm in and take care of both messes. It's a shame, though. I hate wasting food.

Santanos helps me get cleaned up and takes me into the building so I can use the facilities to not feel so gross.

He reaches into his messenger bag and pulls out a big ziploc bag with toiletries in it. He hands me a new toothbrush and a small tube of toothpaste, but he also has a shaving kit, some pads and tampons, and even little bottles of soap and some little square packets that look like big versions of alcohol wipes. I'm glad he's prepared for anything, and while I clean up and brush my teeth, he washes the blood off.

As he is washing his hands, his serious blue eyes stare into mine, and his voice starts sounding a little like a growl. "I'm not sorry for killing that ogre, sweetie. He was hired by the junior Saxon to kill you, and I will never allow anyone to harm you. You're my most precious love, and I will protect you from every threat. It doesn't matter who, when, or where, baby. As long as I'm alive, you will be safe."

I rinse my mouth out and wipe my face before answering. "Even though it makes me sad when people have to die, I'm glad I'm still alive. Thank you for saving me and for wanting to keep me safe. I will probably always get sick when there's a lot of, um, body parts that aren't attached to bodies, but even if I throw up, I am still thankful that you're keeping me safe. And I'm not sorry about Saxon, so you don't have to be sorry about the ogre."

Santanos finishes washing up and drying his hands, and then he pulls on my collar and brings me down for a deep, loving, hot tongue kiss that promises me that he will always take care of me when I need it, and that makes all the bad things that just happened disappear for the rest of the day.

CHAPTER 11

The smell of food welcomes me home after my first day at work. It was a pretty good day after lunch, and I was a little sad that Santanos had to work late, but I'm glad he let me take Gregory, even though he was complaining about wanting to work late too. Thankfully Santanos put his foot down.

Gregory and I put our shoes by the door, and then we go to the main room, carefully avoiding the tables that Oppa collects. Well, I've learned how to walk around them, but Gregory hits a couple.

My grandpas are all here. The big one with black hair is in the living room reading one of Papa's paperbacks, the one that looks like a movie hero is setting the table, and the blue one and the one that's a demon are in the kitchen working together to unpack a bag full of food.

"Do you know my grandpas?" I ask Gregory, hoping I don't have to remember everyone's names; I only remember Grandpa Tag and Grandpa Bear.

"Everyone knows the Patervulpis clan," Gregory grumps, glaring at them.

"Who are you?" Grandpa Tag asks with a really fake smile.

"This is my friend Gregory. Please don't be mean to him; he's already struggling with having enough love inside him because of Santanos eating it. We have to love him so he can heal."

Grandpa Tag's fake smile turns nice and he comes to me, pulling me into a tight hug. "I'm sorry, pupper. Of course we'll help fill him up with love. I didn't realize that Santanos was harming him like that. Maybe you shouldn't work for him if he's hurting his employees."

I sigh and roll my eyes. "No, Grandpa Tag. Santanos needs me so he can't hurt anyone again. I'm feeding him enough, and he can't take enough from me to hurt me. I'm so full of love that I have plenty to share."

Grandpa Tag pats my head. "Of course you are. You're so fucking lovable that it's like having a puppy."

"Is that why everyone keeps calling me pupper?" I didn't make that connection, which makes me feel dumber than usual.

Gregory huffs like he's annoyed, but when I look, his core is trying to shove love out at me. "Of course it is. You're like the most adorable puppy anyone's ever laid eyes on and adopted. Everyone wants to hold you and snuggle you, and you make everyone feel better just by existing in their space."

I release Grandpa Tag and open my arms to Gregory, pushing my love at him so he doesn't have to reach for me. He's not as pretty as Santanos, but he's still so cute and easy to love, especially when he steps into my arms and lets me hold him as he scowls at Grandpa Tag.

I chuckle and kiss the top of his head and hold him close. "I love you so much," I remind him because he needs to hear it a lot.

He grunts and his love pulses happily until Grandpa Tag steps in close and hugs us both. His love surrounds us and even seeps in a little into Gregory even though Gregory puts up a fuss, pushing Grandpa Tag away.

"No, I do not consent to hugs from anyone but the pupper."

I pull him away from Grandpa Tag. "We don't hug people who don't want hugs," I warn him seriously.

Grandpa Tag pouts better than anyone I've ever seen. "Why don't you want my love, Gregory?"

Gregory crosses his arms and glares at him. "Why would I want the love of my enemy? What kind of minion would I be if I fell for the first pretty blue fairy I met?"

Tag's jaw drops and he gasps, grabbing his shirt over his heart. "Who the fuck are you calling a fairy? I am an *elf*. Fairies aren't even from the same realm."

"You look like a fairy. I just thought one of the hunters got a hold of your wings."

"As if I would fall prey to humans even if I was a fairy. Your lot is TSTL." He rolls his eyes and turns on his heels, bouncing back to the kitchen.

Gregory leans against me. "I'm not human," he calls out. "I realize it can be hard to tell for someone of your advanced age, but if you concentrate you'll be able to see I'm a fucking gnome."

"That explains the smell," Grandpa Tag replies with a mean grin.

I sigh again. "You said you would be nice."

"I didn't say I would put up with his rudeness."

I rub Gregory's grumpy guts over his shirt. "You can't blame him when Santanos stole all his love and he's only barely getting back a teeny tiny amount of shine. We don't have to be doormats, Grandpa, but we can be polite even when others are rude. My grandma made sure I knew that—there were a lot of rude kids my age when I was growing up, but I was always polite and I never got into trouble."

Gregory stiffens in my arms and all the grandpas freeze like statues, looking at me with dark expressions.

"Pupper, tell me the truth, do people bully you?" Gregory demands, turning in my arms and pulling my face down so close to his that I can feel his breath on my skin.

I shake my head. "No one here bullies me. There were some people in Fresno, and my sister hates me, but I have a new family now and everyone loves me. I'm happy here, Gregory. My life is full of people who love me now, and I love them too. I've never had so much love in my life as I do now."

He stares at me for another few seconds before releasing his hold on my shirt. "Ok, pupper. If anyone bullies you, you tell me right away. I'm not going to put up with that shit."

I can't help the smile that splits my face, but I remember what Hassan said earlier and what I did, so before I kiss him, I ask, "Can I kiss you now?"

He rolls his eyes and grabs my shirt, pulling me in close and kissing me quickly. He pulls back with a glare. "Good enough?"

I laugh happily and nod. "Yeah. Should I always ask?"

He huffs and shakes his head. "As long as Santanos doesn't mind, you can kiss me and Hassan."

"That's what Hassan said." I laugh and stand up, turning back to a wall of surprise from my grandpas. "What happened?"

"Why are you kissing the enemy?" Grandpa Bear demands, crossing strong arms.

"Gregory isn't *my* enemy," I remind him. "He's my friend, and we're the kind of friends who can kiss and cuddle and love each other."

Gregory snorts and his insides brighten up like he's laughing, but he doesn't say anything so I just keep talking.

"I love you all, but if you're going to hurt Gregory with your words or attitudes, then I'm going to take him home and I'll stay with him until he's feeling better. I thought he was welcome here with me since I'm trying to heal him, but if that's a problem, I won't bring him home with me. I want everyone to be happy." I stop to eye the food the demon grandpa puts on the table. "But please be happy with us here because that food looks really good and I'm very hungry."

I think it's easier to just be honest with everyone about stuff so no one is surprised if you have to leave.

The demon grandpa pulls Grandpa Tag back and puts him in Grandpa Bear's arms. "Pupper, Grandpa Tag is just having a hard time accepting your new friends because we've been on opposite sides of the aisle for a long time. We will learn to get along with Gregory and Hassan and Santanos because we love you, but we might make some mistakes along the way. Especially Dakota, because he's on the council." He points to the grandpa who's reading on the couch and ignoring us.

"Grandpa Dakota isn't the one who's been fighting with Gregory," I point out.

Grandpa Dakota looks up without an expression. "It's because I know how important your friends are, pupper. I don't like Gregory because I've seen the messes he leaves behind when he's being evil. If I read my book, then I won't try to kill him."

"Tch. Gnomes are immune to your thunderbird magic," Gregory replies like we should all know that fact already. He sees my confused expression and explains. "Gnomes' magic works with all kinds of metals, and we're basically metal magic so we can't be electrocuted because we're always grounded, we can't catch fire, things like that."

"Gnomes also have interesting diseases because of their association with metal, like they can get a wasting disease like rust. It's pretty awful," Grandpa Tag says, looking over Gregory like he's looking for the disease.

"We have vaccines now," Gregory informs him, but there's no anger there anymore.

"We know. I was on the team that helped develop it," the demon grandpa says. "Why don't we eat, then we can watch a movie before we head out?"

Gregory grunts and pulls out a chair at the big dining room table and pushes me into it before sitting on my lap just like Santanos does.

I wonder if Santanos told him to sit there or if he likes sitting with me like Santanos does? It doesn't matter because I want him in my lap so I can feed him my love and help him heal. He's very hard to feed love to, but I think it's because he got used to always having Santanos take it out of him, so his soul isn't used to trying to hold it in, and maybe he feels full when he's actually still starving. It's hard to explain, but it just means that I have to feed him slowly and let him get used to being loved and holding love inside him again.

I wrap one arm around his waist and let my love slowly drip out of me into him. "I'm really proud of you," I whisper in his ear.

Gregory shivers and looks at me over his shoulder, raising one eyebrow and scowling at me. "Why?"

"Because you're working hard to refill your love inside you. I can see how hard it is, and I'm proud of you for keeping up the effort when it would be easier to give up. Just like making gains with the weights, you're making gains with the love, and that's something someone should be proud of you for, so I am."

Gregory's love pulses brighter, and he pecks my lips before it dims back down and he turns back around.

Happy that he accepts my encouragement, I turn my attention to getting food in my belly.

"WHAT?" Gregory's shocked question pulls me out of a dead sleep, and I reach for him, pulling him back to be my little spoon.

"Whassamatter?" I mumble, trying to keep my eyes from drifting back to sleep.

"Shh, it's ok; I'm talking to Santanos," he tells me, petting my arm soothingly.

"Mmm," I hum.

"How is that even possible?" Gregory asks, and since he's not talking to me, I just listen to his voice. It's a nice one when he's not being too grumpy.

"We've been working to restore five percent for nearly a hundred years and we've suddenly jumped half a percent in a single day? I repeat: how is that even possible?"

I'm curious about what they're talking about, but I'm too sleepy to do more than sound like a zombie, so I give up trying to stay awake and just decide to wait until tomorrow to ask about it.

THE SECOND MORNING with Gregory goes the same as the first morning. We listen to my wake up music and dance to my happy song and then shower and eat and leave. The taxi we take drops us off at our work building, and then we take the elevator up to the top floor.

I don't remember the conversation from the night before until we get out of the elevator and the pretty demon woman who is the office manager,

Sheila, rushes up to Gregory with a big folder, saying, "This is insane. It's like everyone suddenly decided to do one good deed and it tipped the balance overnight. Except no one is reporting having done a good deed."

"Someone is lying. Someone did something to tip the balance this far and we're going to find out who it is," Gregory growls, sorting through the folder and yelling very loudly, "Someone get me a fucking coffee!"

I grab the back of his neck and make him turn his grumpy face to look at me. "If you ask, I can get you a coffee, and you don't have to yell at anyone else for it. I like helping you, Gregory, and I think Santanos would want me to help you too because you're important to him."

Gregory growls and waves his empty hand in a frustrated movement, but his inner love brightens by a tiny bit. "Ok, pupper. Will you get me a coffee while I go over this report? Hassan would probably like one too, and Santanos usually has a hot chocolate."

I smile, pleased with him, and kiss his forehead to make sure he knows I'm super proud of him. "Good job. I will go get everyone's drinks."

Gregory sighs, pulls my collar down and smacks a kiss on my lips. He lets me go and goes back to reading his report.

Sheila and I share a secret smile, and then I take the stairs down to the break room two floors below us.

Hassan showed me all the best places in the building yesterday, but I didn't get to really come into the breakroom. He was just showing me around, but he did tell me that this is where the best coffee is, which I was surprised to hear because one of the lower floors has a whole coffee bar in it.

The breakroom smells like cleaner and coffee, which is a weird combination, but it must be pretty good because there are a lot of minions in here. Everyone sort of just stops talking when I come in. The kids at school would sometimes do this when they were saying mean things about me, but I haven't met these minions, so they can't possibly be saying mean things.

"Edovard!" My name comes from Erica, the woman in charge of tax evasion.

"Erica! I'm so happy to see you," I tell her, opening my arms up to offer her a hug.

She steps up, gives me a quick hug, and pulls me down to kiss my cheek too. "How was your first day?"

"It was great! I got along with everyone I met and Santanos really liked the idea we had yesterday, and he was very pleased with your progress when Hassan told him about it."

Erica's chest puffs out and she smiles happily as her inner light pulses too.

Before she can say anything, though, I notice someone throwing a bunch of water bottles into the trash can.

"Woah! Dude, what are you doing? We recycle plastics!" I call, heading over to stop him from throwing them in the trash. Except there isn't a recycle bin. "Where are the recycling bins? Why aren't there recycling bins?"

The guy freezes and looks up at me with yellow eyes. He's one of the dark elves my grandma told me were always bad news, but he's got enough love in him that he should understand the importance of recycling. "We don't recycle. I don't even think the building pays for trash service. I think we're on a destroy-the-planet kick."

I know my eyes are as big as dinner plates. "No. We are not doing that. Who is in charge of trash? Why would anyone want to destroy the planet?"

Someone else pipes up—a small person with a floor length beard. "I keep telling these idgits that their plan to take over the world through destruction is pure idiocy, but no one listens to the wizened dwarf, do they?"

"You're trying to take over the world?" I ask, because I'm pretty sure Santanos would have told me about that if it was true.

"Some of us are," one of the lizard people hisses.

I think about that for a second and glance at the empty water bottles. "Ok, but don't you want a world worth taking over? We're evil, but that doesn't mean that we want to live on a trash planet. You can still work toward taking over, but if we recycle and try to leave less of a footprint on the planet, then when we do take it over, we don't have so much work trying to make it a good place for evil to live, right?"

The lizard person's tongue flicks out and the other people talk about it for a minute, and then the guy who was throwing the bottles away starts pulling them back out of the trash, saying, "I just had a thought. What if we started our own recycling plant? We could offer to recycle papers and could probably find a bunch of stuff to blackmail rich companies for money, right? We could make the planet a livable place, and also make millions in blackmail money for our other endeavors."

I point to him. "See, there you go. I bet Erica is really going to like that idea too—do you know her? She's in charge of tax evasion."

Erica laughs and starts helping sort through the trash for recyclables. "I know Dennis. He's got a great mind for insidious planning."

Dennis' inner light beams for Erica. "Thank you. I would be nothing without my partner in crime though," he says and pulls the lizard person to his side, kissing them. "This is Karlesh; he's my mate."

"It's very nice to meet you, Karlesh. I really hope you're having fun trying to take over the world. If I can do anything to help, let me know. If it's something I can do." I glance around, trying not to be embarrassed. "I'm not very good at reading, yet, but I can lift a lot of heavy things."

Karlesh and Dennis both give me matching smiles and their love pulses with the same beat. It's so pretty I can't help but stare at it. "You two really love each other. It's beautiful, you know."

They exchange a look and then smile up at me. "Thank you, Edovard."

Someone else appears at my elbow, holding a tray with four cups on it. She's got long pointy ears and blue hair. "I'm Charlotte. I'm good with drinks, so here's the ones you wanted and an extra for you. It's a soothing tea I think you'll like."

My heart warms with happiness. "Thank you, Charlotte. I really like tea."

She pats my arm as I take the tray. "I know, pupper. Best get back up there."

She's probably right, so I wave goodbye to everyone and head back upstairs.

CHAPTER 12

⚜

"The trash department is going to start a recycling business to help save the planet and blackmail people with their papers," I report as I hand out drinks.

Santanos tilts his head at my news and Gregory and Hassan give me weird looks.

"How did you come across that information?" Santanos asks curiously. "And why haven't I been told about it?"

"Oh! It's because me and Dennis and Karl-something all worked it out together when I went for drinks." I sit on the chair Santanos wants me in and he sits on my lap. "Dennis was throwing away water bottles, so we made a plan for recycling that includes blackmail so it's evil. Evil recycling." I'm pretty proud of that.

Gregory makes a weird noise, and Hassan pats him on the back.

"That's a lovely idea," Santanos laughs, kissing my cheek. "I'm glad you're getting along with the minions."

"I really am. I didn't know if I could get along with evil people, especially because of being an Augur, but so far the only people who I've had magic words about are people who have no love inside them anymore and can't even hold any love anymore. It's really sad that they're like this, but I don't feel so bad about them being murdered when they're killing people first, you know?"

Santanos pets me and holds me tight. "I understand, sweetie. It's sad, but we're trying to make the world a balanced place, and they're shifting the balance the wrong way."

"Exactly—Guilleri Fabian Muir, San Marino, Italy. Three hundred forty-three tourists abducted, one hundred fifty killed, one hundred ninety three ransomed."

Tears fall down my cheeks, and I hug Santanos close because it's so sad how many people this person has hurt.

Santanos holds me close and he repeats what I said into a video, and I know he sends it to the depot without having to see. He loves me so he does that even though it's my job. Sometimes this is a hard job, and I'm really sad and kind of angry that this guy has hurt so many people, but I'm glad that my oppa is going to fix it.

"Oh sweetie. I wish there was something I could do to help," Santanos whispers.

I scrunch my face up and take a deep breath. "It's ok. Someone has to be able to tell my oppa where the really bad guys are, and it's ok that it's me. I don't mind crying for other people. Someone has to. Everyone should be mourned—that's what my grandpa told me when the kids at school made fun of me for crying when they killed a little lizard on the sidewalk."

"Your grandpa sounds like a wise man," Santanos replies.

"He was very smart," I agree, taking the hanky in Santanos' hand and wiping my face with it. "I'm better now. Thank you for telling the depot."

"You're welcome, sweetie."

"If the waterworks are done, can we get back to work?" Gregory demands, waving his big report at us.

Santanos scowls at him. "Unlike you, I haven't gotten to spend the last fifteen hours with my favorite Augur, and I'm hungry. Do you really want me working on empty?"

I examine Santanos core, seeing that he is down a bit on his love, so I open up my heart and let my love flow out of me and into him.

Santanos stiffens in my arms and jerks around, pulling me straight into a tingly warm kiss so full of love that it feels like I'm pulling it into my core instead of pushing it into his.

He moans into my mouth and shifts until he's straddling me, and that makes the tingles just explode everywhere all over me. It's so big and so new and it feels so good that I can't help how tight I hold him. I can't get close enough and I'm frustrated, but I can't tell why until Santanos' hands wriggle under my shirt and I realize that I hate that I can't feel his skin against mine.

I jerk back from the kiss and freeze, staring at him with wide eyes until I remember that Santanos probably would let me take off our shirts so we can have skin-hugs. He'd probably like it, but I won't know unless I ask.

"Can we take off our shirts? I think I want to kiss you and hug you skin-to-skin."

Santanos' smile is as bright as his inner light. "Of course, baby. I love being naked with you."

"This is so unfair," Gregory grumbles, breaking into our conversation.

I frown at him, not sure why he's upset, but I don't like it. "What's not fair?"

Gregory glares at me and Santanos. "I haven't gotten to have sex in days. I haven't gone this long without sex for a hundred years, and I need it. I'm going to go crazy if I don't get an orgasm soon."

Thankfully, Santanos doesn't make me figure out how to fix this since I've got nothing to do with sex. "There's no reason you can't get fucked, Gregory. I just have to make sure I'm not eating from you while you do it."

Gregory narrows his eyes at me. "Is that true? I can have sex?"

I shrug. "Yes? As long as sex doesn't take love out of your core, there's no reason you can't."

Hassan suddenly knocks Gregory's papers out of his hand and shoves him back onto the couch, kissing him like he's eating him.

My eyebrows try to reach my hair line and a big ol' smile cracks my face as I watch their love get as bright as the sun. I look at Santanos, just as happy as can be. "Sex is really good for their love," I whisper as I help him untie his tie.

"Sex is good for the soul under normal circumstances," Santanos agrees, working on unbuttoning his shirt. "If you ever want to try it, I want to be your first, ok? You don't have to choose me, but I would like it if you did."

I chuckle and pull my own shirt off, excited to get skin-to-skin with him. "I wouldn't choose anyone else. Well, I might have asked Gregory or Hassan, but if you want me to ask you, I will. I'm not ready yet, but I think I might be soon. Kissing you does make my penis feel bigger."

Santanos sucks in a breath and forgets about his shirt, so I help him get it all the way off and then pull him chest-to-chest with me.

"Oh yeah, that's better," I mumble to myself, relieved to be so close to him.

"I would pay to watch you with Gregory and Hassan," he whispers, glancing at the two guys on the couch, who are now naked.

"They got all of their clothes off faster than you got your shirt off," I tease Santanos, running my big hand up and down the creamy skin on his back. I love the feel of his softness. He's not muscular like me and Hassan, but I love how he feels. I'm hard and he's soft, and it's perfect when we're this close. "Kisses again," I mutter, because that was the point of taking off our shirts.

<Me: Um, should I skip this part?

Santanos: Don't you dare. I want to hear what it was like for you.

Papa: More importantly, the people reading your book want to know all about Santanos' sexy times game.

Santanos: Who says I was ever playing with this boy?>

Santanos gives me what I want and pushes in close, pressing our mouths together again. His tongue slides against mine, and I think I'm getting better at this, because not only does my love just burst open to feed him, but the tingles that always happen get even more intense. It's like I'm filling up with love and at the same time filling him up too, and my body loves how it makes my soul feel when we do this.

Santanos moans again and then pulls back, staring at me with heavy eyes and shiny lips. "I need to come, Edovard."

I shudder at the sound of my name on his angelic lips. I didn't even know it could sound that way. "Where should I bring you?" I ask. Why do we have to stop kissing to go somewhere?

"No, baby. I need to orgasm. Is it ok if I take my cock out?"

Ooooooh. Right. I try to remember everything Bellamy told me, but honestly, just seeing Hassan putting his penis inside Gregory's butt reminds me what Santanos really needs.

"Yes, ok. Maybe you should show me how to use my hand on you?" I think that would be ok.

Santanos shudders and nods. "If you want me to. Don't force yourself, my love."

"No, I won't. I want to do this. It's important to you and I love you and want you to feel important to me."

Santanos nods. "Of course, baby. I'll help you learn."

He opens his pants and pulls his penis out. It's hard and long, but not as big as mine, and a different shape too. Mine is thick at the bottom and pointed like an arrow at the top, but his is slender with two little bumps on the underside and a horn that sticks out from his short, blond pubic hair that's shaped like the top of a heart. I've never seen anything like it, but most amazing is that he doesn't even have any balls at all.

<Papa: OMG. Is your penis shaped differently than humans?

Santanos: Not enough that a human would notice when he's flaccid, but when he's hard it's enough different that there would have been questions.

Bellamy: I could go the rest of my life without hearing about how differently shaped the penises are in my family.>

I touch his little horn and Santanos sucks in another breath, shivering. "Oh that's good."

"What is it?" I ask, rubbing it again and getting the same reaction from him.

"It's my—" he makes a noise that doesn't sound anything like English. "It stimulates a clitoral orgasm for those who have sex with women. Please keep touching it. It's been a while since it popped out."

I slide my big finger around it, and when Santanos makes a noise like he really likes something, I do it again, and then he grabs my shoulder and his penis shoots out white stuff—whatever Bellamy called it—and for some reason I feel like I just did the most amazing thing I've ever done. Santanos keeps throbbing for a little while, and when he's done my chest is covered in his stuff, but I don't mind because his inner light is amazing. He's happy and content, full of love, and the look on his face is like hot chocolate and a cozy quilt and a full belly all at once.

<Grand Sugar Daddy: Let no one say my baby's descriptions don't paint a vivid picture.>

If this is what sex is like, I want to do it all the time. I love the way Santanos looks right now, how he feels. He's so beautiful that I don't want to look away. I want him to look like this all the time.

I quickly wipe up his stuff from my stomach with a tissue off his desk, and then I pull him in for a warm hug, holding his relaxed self safe and secure. It's only when I get him settled that I notice that Gregory and Hassan are also cuddling on the couch, and I wish that there was a nice big bed like the one in the hotel room so that we could all cuddle together. It'd feel good to have them close too. We could share all the love and spread it around so that everyone is getting enough.

Maybe I should get a bigger bed for my room so everyone can come sleep with me. I wonder how much that would cost?

CHAPTER 13

⁂

"Sweetpea." Santanos' pet name stops me from staring in amazement at the ceiling of the church he brought me to. It looks like a cartoon of angels and humans and lots of amazing artwork. Well, not a cartoon. It's definitely a painting, but it's very colorful.

We came here through a portal, traveling all the way across the world just to be here.

<Oppa: The number of illegal portals you have access to astounds me sometimes.

Gregory: *laughs* You don't know the half of it.

Hassan: I'm a shaman.

Santanos: His magic is about a quarter of the reason I hired him initially.

Me: What's the rest?

Santanos: His body, his mind, and his soul.

Me: Awww.

Papa: Sigh. It is ridiculously sweet.>

I focus back on Santanos and not on the colorful ceiling because we're here to work. "What do I do now?" I ask.

"Before I met you, I would bring about fifty minions with me to have sex around me so I could eat their energy and power up, so to speak, but since you've told me that is unhealthy for my minions, I'm going to need you to do the job. I'm interviewing several candidates for the position that Bellamy abandoned when Romily claimed him, and I expect at least a few of them to try to cash in on one of the contracts currently floating around offering to pay for my demise."

My brow scrunches, but before I can ask my phone what demise means, Hassan says, "His death. Some people have offered to pay others to kill Santanos."

My breath rushes into me and it almost feels like I'm choking, but Santanos leans into me and pets my chest. "It's ok, my love. No one can actually kill me. I've got you here and a ward that keeps me safe. Honestly, I would be fine all on my own, but I'm terrible at sitting back passively, so I need you here to help me in case I decide to do something aggressive. All you have to do is feed me like you already do."

I swallow and hug him tight, and Hassan points to the throne where I'm supposed to sit with Santanos, so I take him there and sit with him on my lap, protecting him with my big body. No wait, I should be in front of him, right?

"You should sit behind me," I decide, grabbing him to stand again.

"No." That word stops me. "All I need you to do is feed me. I don't want you to shield me. I already have a ward, and Gregory and Hassan are going to help me keep you safe."

They stand on each side of me, scowling out at the empty church, while I hold Santanos in my lap. Since I'm not in charge, and I've been given my job, I open up my core and start pushing my love into Santanos. It's super easy, and he just takes it all inside him because he's the best at receiving love.

Santanos sighs and relaxes into me. He reaches over and takes Gregory's hand, and then Hassan puts his hand on my shoulder, and it feels like we're all sharing our feelings with each other. Not really, but we're connected even if I'm the only one feeding Santanos.

Since I have plenty to share, I start pushing trickles into Gregory and Hassan too. It doesn't matter how much I give away; I've been so full of love all my life that I have more than enough to give away, and I get my love refilled all the time when people like Erica and Papa and the Grandpas give me their love too. Even Gregory and Hassan add to the love in my core even though I'm feeding them. Sometimes they pulse with extra and that helps me stay strong and healthy too.

"Here comes the first candidate," Gregory whispers just before a dark shadow walks into the church.

It's weird. It's pretty bright in here, but the person coming toward us is like a ninja. They're one with the shadows or something because the light doesn't really touch them. I can't tell what they look like, but Santanos seems ok, so I just watch and listen.

"I got your invitation," the shadow says, but their voice isn't very loud, and I wish they would speak up so I can hear them better, but they don't. "To what do I owe this dubious pleasure?"

"The pleasure I induce is never dubious, Pat," Santanos replies smoothly. "I'm known for always leaving my bedmates quite deliciously satisfied."

"That's true," I accidentally say. "Sorry."

Santanos turns and gives me a lovely smile. "You're welcome to speak, Edovard."

For some reason when he says my name the tingles that I get from feeding him make me shudder and my skin breaks out in goosebumps like I'm cold.

He turns back to Pat. "This sweet boy is my new assistant. I'm currently in the process of replacing some of the employees I've lost over the last year. You're here because I need a new assassin. My precious boy's brother left me in the lurch a few months ago."

I nod. I heard about how Papa stole Bellamy from Santanos. I thought it was a little rude to just take him away, but Bellamy is happier being a Foxily, and that's more important than how he was stolen.

"So I'm here for you to offer me the job?" Pat asks as Gregory motions for them to stop walking toward us; they're pretty far away still.

Santanos waves his hand like he's trying to wave away a fart, but what happens is he knocks a stick right out of the air! I didn't even see it coming—it's not a stick, it's an arrow like from a bow and arrow.

Even though Santanos stopped it from hurting any of us, he barely even looks at it and just keeps on talking. "Of course not. You're here because I invited you for an interview. If you're interested in becoming the Avatar of Evil's official assassin, we'll have a conversation. If you pass the initial interview, you will join the rest of the candidates in a competitive hunt, and the winner of the competition will be awarded the job."

As soon as Santanos is done talking, Hassan shoots a gun, which isn't as loud as I expected, but I think it's probably because of the thing on the end that makes it less loud (I don't know what they're called). A few seconds later, some guy appears out of nowhere and limps out the door, leaving a trail of blood behind him.

After he leaves, I turn my eyes back to Pat, who is completely dark all around the outside, and pretty dark on the inside, but nothing I couldn't make better if they wanted help. They don't move, and I still can't see what they look like, but the way they stand there makes me relax a little. They weren't the one who shot at us, after all.

"I think you'd make a good assassin for Santanos," I tell them so that they have someone encouraging them to be their best self. "The minions would like you because your outfit is so cool, and your insides fit in with all the rest of them too. If you joined us, you would get a lot of love and I could help your love core get healthy. You probably feel like not a lot of people love you right now, but if you won the competition and joined us, you'd get a nice family who would fill you up with all the good feelings and you wouldn't feel so gray anymore."

Pat doesn't move a muscle and they don't say anything for a while, which makes me squirm. I don't like it when people stare at me after I talk. It usually means I said something they think is stupid, and I hate that.

Gregory lets go of Santanos' hand and pats my head, and Hassan steps forward half a step. Santanos reaches up and grips Hassan's wrist, and since I don't know what is happening, but it's making me feel a little sick, I just hug Santanos tighter and push my nose into his neck to smell him so I don't have to look at Pat anymore. The sage smell is very comforting.

"You've made my precious assistant uncomfortable, and under different circumstances with a different assistant that would be fine, but in this case, you've pissed off my bodyguards as well, which has disqualified you unless there's an apology forthcoming. You may leave," Santanos tells them, reaching back to hold my neck and firmly trap me right where I am.

It makes me love him even more than I already do.

"I see," Pat says, and that's the last thing I hear until there's another voice.

"Hello beloved leader!" the loud, joyful voice makes me jerk up to see a big man walking in wearing a dress like the Romans used to wear.

Santanos' voice is warm when he replies, "Hello Brutus, how happy I am to see you."

"To what do I owe the delight of your invitation?" Brutus asks, stopping exactly where Pat stood. He has two long braids that he pulls forward and then he reaches into his dress and pulls out a pipe and a bag of something to smoke. I can't tell from here if it's tobacco or marijuana.

"I am looking to hire a new assassin," Santanos explains, and then tells Brutus the same thing he told Pat.

I really like Brutus because as happy as he sounds, his inner light is even happier. He is full of love and joy and I know if he wins he's going to be a good addition to our workplace.

Brutus lights his pipe and the scent of tobacco wafts toward us while he and Santanos talk. At the end Brutus agrees to join the competition and then he leaves.

I sigh and kiss Santanos' hair. "He would make a good minion."

"You would think that," Santanos giggles. "But he's currently trying to figure out how to cash in on the contracts."

"What?" I don't believe it.

"He started his career as a professional assassin by killing a famous ruler. He's going to join the competition, but not before he figures out if it's possible to kill me now or if he needs to win the competition in order to do it later," Santanos explains.

"Well then don't hire him," I whisper emphatically just in case Brutus can hear me.

Santanos laughs again. "It's ok. He can't kill me. He can try, and I will admire his dedication to a lost cause, but he can't actually do it."

I'm not sure how I feel about hiring someone who's going to betray us. "I hope someone who doesn't want to kill you wins," I decide.

Santanos leans back and kisses me, and then another person walks in.

"Hello, you gorgeous specimen of evil," she calls over the clack of her bright red heels on the tile floor. She's wearing a strapless dress and black pantyhose and her lips are painted the same color as her dress.

"Wow," I blurt out. "I really like your matching dress and lips."

She takes off her sunglasses and winks at me. "Thank you, sweetie pie. I appreciate a man who knows how to compliment a queen."

"You're a queen? From where? I don't think we should hire a queen, right? That would be hard because you have to do your queen stuff and can't just go around killing people."

The woman bursts out laughing, which shuts me up fast. "Oh sweetie, aren't you just adorable? I'm not a queen like the ruler of a nation. I'm a drag queen. Well, on Saturday nights I'm a drag queen; the rest of the time I'm a size queen, if you know what I mean." She winks again, but I don't know what she means and I think I better shut up again.

"Priscilla, meet Edovard. He's my new assistant. It would be in everyone's best interest if we all understand that Edovard is precious to me and loved by Hassan and Gregory as well," Santanos says, but there's something in his voice that makes the hair on the back of my neck stand up.

Priscilla's eyes widen and she backs up a step. "Of course, obviously. He's adorable; why wouldn't you love him? Edovard, it's very nice to make your acquaintance. I'm Priscilla Jefferson; sometimes I like to be called Mikey, and I'll let you know if I want you to call me that."

"Ok. Thank you. Nice to meet you," I tell her and then let Santanos push my nose back into his neck. It's comfortable here anyway. Plus, Priscilla is very gray inside and I kind of just want to look at Santanos for a while. Grays make me sad sometimes.

Santanos and Priscilla talk, and then the next person comes in and I can tell right away that this is the person I want to be Santanos' assassin.

He's wearing one of those orange and red robes that some movies use as costumes for the monks from Asia, except it's not like the movies, and there's pretty beads on it and some frills. He's bright, not like me but pretty close, and his smile is kind, and when he introduces himself it's like listening to a summer rain and the wind in the trees and a fire crackling—his voice is very soothing. "My name is Gaanbatar Batbayar. I received my master's invitation to this job interview. Batbayar Ganbold."

"This is the one," I whisper to Santanos. I can't look away from him, he's almost as beautiful as Santanos is.

Santanos tightens his grip on my neck and lets me know he heard me with a soft hum. "Hello, Gaanbatar. I am Santanos, the Avatar of Evil. I've known your master for nearly a hundred years and have heard many stories of your successes over the years. Welcome."

Amusement makes the wrinkles around his dark eyes come out. "I am sure he enjoyed telling of my failures as well. Thank you for your welcome."

"He does take particular delight in those as well. Tell me, why did he pass his invitation on to you?" Santanos asks.

Gaanbatar freezes up for a moment, and his inner light takes on a sad hue. I squeeze Santanos as Gaanbatar explains because I know what that means before he tells us. "My master passed on to the next life a few years ago, and I have taken up his legacy."

Santanos hums softly and his inner light also takes on a similar hue of grief. "I am pained to hear that, Gaanbatar. I loved Batbayar for many years."

"He always spoke highly of you too."

Santanos thanks him and they move on to the interview, and thankfully Gaanbatar accepts the invitation to the challenge.

Before he leaves, I speak up to make sure he knows I'm rooting for him. "Mr. Gan But Ar, I want you to win. You're the right person for this job. Please work hard so you win."

He gives me his kind smile and dips his head slightly. "I will, pupper."

My eyes widen as he slips out and I look at Santanos, "How did he know that's what my family calls me?"

"I would also like to know how he knew that," Gregory announces, glaring suspiciously at where Gaanbatar left.

"He's a Mongolian monk in the tradition of Tengri; the stones probably told him what your family calls you," Hassan explains and then gives me a serious look. "Are you sure you want him, Edovard? There are no secrets from a Tengri monk like him. The very air whispers to him."

I take a deep breath and trust my gut like my grandma always told me to. "He's the right one. I can tell."

Santanos and Hassan exchange a glance, and one by one all three of them give me kisses. Santanos presses his lips to mine last and pulls back. His pretty blue eyes distract me for a moment, but he helps me focus again when he speaks. "Ok, sweetie. He's the one."

My heart fumbles in my chest and catches all my emotions before they hit the ground. Sometimes I don't know why I feel the things I feel, especially when the emotions are complicated, but I know the reason this time. "Thank you for trusting me. Not a lot of people trust me because I'm not too smart, but I know I'm right this time."

Santanos' confidence sinks right into me and makes me feel how much he loves me. "I know you are too, my love. We're done interviewing. Hassan has arranged a tour of Rome for us and then we'll eat at a delicious little bistro that's Gregory's favorite here. The regional cuisine they offer is fabulous, and he wants to share your first experience with Roman cuisine with you."

"That makes me feel very important," I tell Gregory so he knows how much I appreciate him. "Thank you."

Gregory grumbles, but he leans down and kisses me again.

When he straightens back up, Santanos stands, so I do too, but I turn to Hassan since he did something for me too (I'm really looking forward to getting a tour of Rome). I don't think he needs words as much as he needs actions, so I just kiss him to say thank you. His insides warm up, which is different from the bright pulses that he sometimes has when I make him feel loved. It's him feeling love toward me, and it makes my love feel gooey, but I don't say anything because I learned not to tell people when they loved me a long time ago.

Grandma made that lesson stick, but I don't like to think about that, so I don't.

<Papa: Is this one of those things we're going to talk about later?

Me: I don't like to talk about that kind of thing.

Santanos: Remember how we talked about it being important to share our burdens?

Me: Yeah, I remember. I'll tell you about it after I'm done talking to the computer.

Papa: Thank you for trusting us, pupper.>

I do like to think about food and good company and all the love I have in my life, so I hold Santanos' hand and Gregory's, and Hassan leads us out of the church with the ceiling painted like an animated movie, and I choose to enjoy all the warm thoughts that I get to have along with this adventure.

CHAPTER 14

"Where are you?" Bellamy asks through the speaker on Santanos' phone because I forgot to charge mine and it died.

It's not my fault. There were a lot of exciting things happening today, and I forgot to plug it in. Everyone makes mistakes, and that's ok.

"We're currently enjoying the nightlife of Rome." Santanos sounds like a cat that caught the canary, and the smile on his face looks as wicked as that old cat from the cartoons.

"Edovard is supposed to be home by dinner time," Bellamy reminds us.

"I forgot about that," I admit. "I was really excited because we were going to Italy and I've never been. Is it ok if I stay? It's really interesting here and Santanos is going to take me to an underground dance club. I'm a really good dancer."

Gregory leans over and speaks into the phone. "He is an exceptional dancer. Better than anyone I've ever danced with." He says that and snickers as he sits back in his seat.

A warm feeling fills me up at the compliment as Bellamy responds dryly. "Papa would like to know when you had the opportunity to dance with our pupper."

"I dance with him in the mornings," I explain. "It's a good way to get the grumpy guts out."

There's a pause on the other side and then Oppa's voice asks, "Are you safe, healthy, and happy?"

Something that sounds a lot like the crash of someone breaking one of Oppa's tables disrupts the conversation, but no one says anything, so I tell him, "I am safe, happy, and super healthy, and Gregory and Hassan are getting better all the time, and Santanos is healthy and happy and he loves me." They all do, but I don't know if I should tell Gregory and Hassan that.

"I do," Santanos tells Oppa.

Oppa's voice sounds like a threat when he says, "Bring my pup home whole."

I expect Santanos to giggle, but he growls something in a language I don't know, and Oppa replies and then they end the call.

I stare at him hoping he will tell me what they said without making me ask because it's rude to intrude on a private conversation, but it's also rude to have a private conversation in front of people. My grandma did it all the time with my grandpa and my sister. I didn't learn the same language they did and when they didn't want me to know what they were saying, they would speak in Greek. Even though no one told me, I figured it out on my own that it's rude to talk about people right in front of them when they can't understand your words.

Santanos kisses my lips. "There's a promise in the language of our people that is more meaningful than any promise made in English. I was just telling him that you would be safe with me."

"Oh." I guess it's ok if he's doing something to make Oppa feel better. "My new family kinda struggles with you, but it's only because they can't see what a good man you are."

He giggles, shaking with laughter and getting bright inside him. "I think you're the only person alive who has the capacity to call the Avatar of Evil a good man."

"You're full of love and light. You make me feel the same way that holiday lights make me feel during the winter, and the way a hot cup of tea makes me feel when I'm upset. You're good, and I love you, and the only person who can convince me that you're a bad person is you. You're like that character from that game movie. Just because you're the leader of the bad guys doesn't mean you're a bad person." I thought I'd already made that clear.

Santanos looks at me like he wants to eat me and kisses me with hard lips. He pushes his tongue into my mouth and tastes every part of it. My heart starts pounding in my chest like I'm on a treadmill, and then the tingles hit me like I ran out in the middle of traffic without looking both ways. My penis feels like it grows as big as the Grinch's heart, and then his grip on me gets really tight so I can't escape when all the feelings get too big.

The sound that bursts out of me isn't big or even loud, but it freezes him. His tongue slides back into his mouth and he helps me calm down with smaller kisses and gentle pets up and down my neck and arms.

"You are a treasure," he whispers, kissing my neck under my ear.

I shiver and goosebumps spread out over my skin, starting right where his lips touch me. For some reason I feel like I should apologize, but I didn't do anything wrong, did I?

My eyes start stinging like they want to cry, and my nose tightens and makes breathing a little bit harder. "Why do I feel bad?"

"Oh sweetie," Santanos whispers.

Suddenly Gregory and Hassan both have their hands on me, petting me like Santanos, and they all surround me in a big, tight hug that makes the tears spill out, but also helps me not need to cry too much.

"There's nothing wrong with not wanting too many kisses," Santanos assures me.

"I like your kisses!" I exclaim, feeling even worse for some reason.

"I know, my love. I know you like kisses, but you don't like them too much, and I made you feel bad when I kissed you for too long."

"No—that's not—" It doesn't sound quite right, but I don't know the words that would make it right.

"Do you feel like you've disappointed Santanos because the kiss was too long for you?" Gregory asks, sounding soft for the first time since I've met him.

His words feel right and the tears in my eyes spill again. "Yeah. I think that's right. I don't want to feel like it's too big when you want to keep going."

Santanos' grip on me tightens and he pushes his face in close so he can look me in the eyes. "You did not disappoint me. I like you how you are, including the part of you that gets overwhelmed by kissing me and enforces your boundaries and limits. I love all the parts of you, and sometimes I want to show you that, but I'm still learning the best ways to show you. Everyone likes different things, and I'm still learning what you like."

That makes sense, but it feels selfish. "But I want to do the things you like, too." They're just sometimes scary. Although watching him feeling really good and giving him a nice orgasm was a good feeling for me. I liked that a lot.

"You absolutely do, sweetie pie. You do."

I take a deep breath and remember that. I make my brain accept it and then I feel better. I nod at Santanos and kiss his lips, then I give Gregory a kiss too and then Hassan. They're important too.

"Better?" Santanos checks.

I nod quickly. "Yes. I'll remember that you're not disappointed in me next time and that you like me just the way I am."

"Good, because it's disturbing when the happiest guy I've ever met cries," Gregory grumps, but his grip on me is tighter than both Hassan's and Santanos'. He was definitely the most worried, but I shouldn't tell him that.

He wouldn't like being called out like that.

<Papa: *How did you hide the soft-hearted evil little gnome you are from us?*
Gregory: *At what point am I allowed to kill him?*
Me: *Please don't kill my family. I only just found them.*
Gregory: **grumble* Only because it's you.*>

I kiss him again. "I'm sorry I worried you."

Oops.

Gregory turns a funny shade of red and shakes me a little. "I wasn't worried. I was disturbed."

I laugh, feeling lighter and happier than I did before. "Ok. I'm sorry I disturbed you."

Hassan doesn't laugh, but his insides light up like they do when he's amused.

Santanos giggles, and then Gregory knocks on the window and the door to the limo opens.

The driver stands by the door while we all get out, and then Hassan leads us down a set of stairs and through a red door. Music thumps as we pay the cover and Hassan talks to the bouncer. We head into the club proper, and I follow Hassan up to the VIP section as I look around. The music is new to me, but I really like it. It makes my body want to move. It's not really crowded like some of the clubs in California would get (I only went when someone invited me and paid for it because clubbing is super expensive), and I like that I'm not going to have a hard time finding room on the dance floor.

As soon as we claim our spots in the private area, Santanos orders a bottle of some kind of drink for us to share, but I'm too excited about dancing to stay here. I can't even sit down, and I grab Gregory's hand before he can.

"Dance with me!" I shout, even though the sound isn't as loud in here as it is down on the dance floor.

Gregory shoots Santanos a look, and Santanos waves us off. "I'll come down after a drink or two. I need to speak to Giana first."

Excited, I drag Gregory down to the dance floor and into the crowd. Our bodies move together like we've had years of practice dancing together. He follows my lead, and then for the next song lets me follow his lead. It's so much fun, but it gets hot and sweaty pretty fast. A couple of girls dance over to us, and since they're as excited as I am about being here, I pull them in to dance with us too. Gregory raises one brow, asking without asking why he would want to dance with a stranger, but I just kiss him and push him toward one of the girls.

He seems satisfied with that, and we both dance with the girls for a couple of songs. When they leave, a guy who looks like I could do a bicep curl with him and a chubby girl come over. Gregory shoots me another look but doesn't argue with me and just pulls the guy in, grinding up on him.

I laugh, taking the girl's hand and dancing with her. She's soft when she dances close, and her inner joy is so bright. I really enjoy having her as a partner too.

After those two leave—they start kissing on the dancefloor and then get excited and leave without even saying goodbye—three men come over to me and Gregory. Two of them are ok. They don't have a lot of love inside them, but they're not as bad as Gregory. The third one's insides are pitch black. He has a slimy smile and tries to grind on me, but I don't like how he feels or looks.

I don't want to dance with him, and suddenly Gregory is right there, putting himself between me and the guy. The other two think we're doing a group dance and surround us, making me feel trapped. One of them grabs my butt, which shouldn't surprise me because the girls I was dancing with before did the same, but this doesn't feel right. There's something not right about the three guys surrounding me and Gregory.

With as pitch black as the one guy is, I'm surprised the magic doesn't give me his name and a list of his—crimes? I don't know if it's breaking the law so much as just evil acts. But that's not right either, is it? Because Gregory and Hassan do evil things and the magic doesn't want them dead. Well, they don't do things that are so evil that they tip the balance the wrong way, and I'm surprised this guy hasn't done that because of how black his core is. I guess if he ever does, the magic will tell someone to kill him, but until then, I don't want to be around him.

"Thirsty!" I holler over the music so Gregory knows I want to leave.

Gregory is dancing—well, he was dancing, but now he's just standing between me and the evil guy—with his back to my front, and when he hears me say that, he grabs my hand and steps toward the bar.

As soon as Gregory isn't standing between us, the evil guy crowds in too close and wraps me up in his arms, speaking loudly in my ear. "Let your bodyguard go and dance with me, sexy. I can give you the night of your life." He presses his erection against me.

My heart starts pounding in my chest and fear freezes me. My mouth tastes like pennies and the need to pee becomes the most important thing about my dick. I try to back away from him, but the other two guys are right there, pushing me back into him.

"No," I whisper. I want to shout it, but my throat is too tight.

Gregory tries to pull me out of the circle, but someone yanks his hand out of mine.

The evil guy puts his mouth on mine, and I jerk away, but the other two push me into him again and he grabs my face and forces me to stay still.

His mouth makes me feel like throwing up, and I hate the slimy feel of his touch. It's like the blackness in his heart is spreading over my skin. It's so gross and so disgusting that I start to feel sick, but then, thankfully, he's gone.

Santanos rips him off me and throws him into the rest of the dancers, who get out of the way quickly and let him fall to the floor.

The other two guys disappear from behind me, and when I glance back, Hassan and Gregory have them in choke holds. I take a deep breath and push up against Santanos' back. I shudder at the memory of the guy's hands on me.

Why doesn't the magic want him dead?

A couple of big guys grab the guy off the floor and drag him over to Santanos. A tall woman with a concerned look on her face walks up too, and she and Santanos talk to the guy for a minute before the bouncers walk him out of the club.

Santanos takes my hand and leads me back up to the VIP section. He pushes me onto one of the sofas and hands me a tall glass of water that I drink down. He refills it, hands it back to me, then turns to talk to the woman. "I want his name. Every scrap of information you can get in the next ten minutes."

"Are you going to have him killed?" she laughs, sitting in one of the chairs with the grace of a ballerina.

Santanos pets my curly, sweaty hair. "I've just interviewed the candidates I'm considering to replace the assassin Fox's Harbinger stole from me. This will be a fantastic way to cull them down."

The woman's smile is as beautiful as an angel's but as scary as a monster's. "Fun." She stands up and her silver gown swirls around her when she turns. "I'll email you in ten minutes."

She leaves, and Santanos turns back to me. "That man will be dead in an hour. Let's hope Gaanbatar wins the job."

It's like a wave of knowing and relief crashes into me. My heart calms down and all the fear that made me freeze on the dancefloor slides away. "He will. I know it." And I do. I can't explain why, but I know Gaanbatar is going to win.

CHAPTER 15

The best part of magic is that we can just step through some doorways and end up on the other side of the world without having to fly on Thunderbirds or in airplanes. Thunderbirds are really hard to fly on. I found that out when I met my new dads. Oppa can turn into one, and flying with him makes me sick and tires me out.

When we get done at the club in Rome, we go back to the place where the doors are, and we walk back to Santanos' office building. It was fun to visit, but I'm glad to be back.

<Oppa: Just how many illegal portals do you have?

Santanos: Enough to keep you on your toes for centuries.>

Oh! I bet my bed was delivered while I was gone. I sent Grandpa Tag a video message and he said he would wait for it.

I bring my phone out while Santanos and Gregory get some reports from the minions and Hassan does whatever he does, and I call Bellamy.

"Hello, pupper. Are you back?"

"Yes, we just got back. Did my bed get delivered? Can you check my room?"

"I don't have to; I was here when the furniture guys got here. We moved the old bed out and the new bed in." I like his accent in my ears. He has a nice, soothing voice.

"Thank you. Is it ok if Santanos, Gregory, and Hassan sleep over tonight?"

Bellamy doesn't answer right away, which makes me nervous, but then he asks, "Are you sleeping with all three of them?"

"I've only slept with Gregory, but I want them all with me. It doesn't feel right to just have Gregory over every night. Hassan misses him, and I want Santanos with me. It's just easier if everyone is in the same bed, so I got a really big one." It makes sense in my head; besides, it would be better if we all cuddled together after sex. I might not be ready for sex yet, but they were all in love before I even came along, and they shouldn't have to stop just because I'm here now. It's not fair, and Santanos told me that he's not disappointed in me. It's ok if I just give Santanos orgasms without…*you know*.

I don't need those kinds of touches.

"Wait, pupper. Let me make sure I understand before I tell you what to do. Are you going to fuck Gregory, Hassan, and Santanos in your new bed?"

For some reason his question makes me blush even though I was just thinking about this too. "No. I don't—I'm not—I don't need that. If they want to it's fine by me. I just want them close so I can heal their love—well, Gregory and Hassan—and I love Santanos. I want him with me all the time. It's not like…*you know*."

"You do know that Santanos is an incubaccha. He needs sex."

"I know that. He's not not getting what he needs," I whisper.

"Ok. I'll let the dads know that you're bringing home the enemy. Our family is so fucked up."

I huff at that. "Our family might not be like the ones we grew up in, but it's not bad. I like it."

Bellamy laughs. "Yeah. It's not so awful I want to run away, even if you've decided to keep the Avatar of Evil."

Something clicks into place inside me when he says that. "That's exactly right. Santanos is mine. He belongs to me and I belong to him, but I also belong to our family, so he belongs to our family too."

"I'm going to let you explain that to Papa. This is the best birthday present ever." Bellamy chuckles when he says that.

JENNIFER CODY

"Is it your birthday?" I didn't know and I didn't get him a present, but Santanos will let me if—

"Not for a few more weeks. I'll make sure you know when my birthday really is. Papa's is on Christmas, though. That's pretty easy to remember."

Whew. "Yeah. I can remember that."

"Ok, pupper, see you soon. Be careful with yourself and get home safely. We love you."

"I love you too." I love being in a family that says that a lot. It's nice not to have to hide my heart from them when they make it feel so full of goodness.

We both say goodbye, and I end the call. When I look over, Gregory and Santanos have their heads together reading a thick report while a couple of minions stand next to them holding hands and looking nervous.

Their inner lights look a little dull, so I go over and stand behind the minions, opening my arms and bending to whisper close to their ears. "My arms are available for minion hugs if you want them. You don't have to have hugs, but sometimes it makes us feel better when we're feeling nervous."

Neither of them says anything, but they both step back and let me wrap my arms around their shoulders. I let my love trickle into them, just kind of letting them soak in it rather than trying to feed it to them. It helps them feel better and that helps with their insides.

Santanos looks up at me, glances at the minions, then just sort of stares at me for a moment before murmuring, "Gregory."

Gregory looks up from the papers with a confused look and a grumpy frown, and then he looks at me too. His gaze bounces back to Santanos, who keeps staring at me, so I smile at him and hug the minions tighter so I don't forget they need me right now. I'd rather be holding Santanos, but that's not fair to these two.

Gregory's eyes narrow at me and then he stops looking confused and looks suspicious. "Pupper, are you loving the minions?"

I laugh at that question and kiss both the minions on top of their heads. "Of course I am. They were very nervous while you were looking at their work. They need someone to tell them they're doing their jobs well and that they're very good at being minions. Look how happy they are now." And people think I ask dumb questions.

Gregory glances at the minions and then looks at Santanos. "You don't think…?"

Santanos hums softly and his pretty smile makes me feel squishy inside. Warm and happy. I love it when he smiles at me. "I do, but let's keep this to ourselves. Edovard, my love, Silas and Becky are doing their jobs perfectly, and I am pleased with their reports. Please keep us informed, you two. Your reports are vital to our work."

Silas and Becky pulse brightly at the compliment from their boss. They tell Santanos a few more things, and he asks some questions, and then everyone is done, so they both give me an extra squeeze and go back to wherever they usually work.

Once they're gone, I pick Santanos up because it feels like a long time since I've gotten to hold him, even though it hasn't been. "I bought a really big bed so everyone can come sleep at my house. I think it's better for Gregory to have us all there, and I don't want you to be away from me all night again. You're mine and I'm yours, and we shouldn't be sleeping in different beds anymore."

Santanos grins wickedly, but he's so happy it's hard to see it through his brightness. "Oh sweetie. Are you asking us to move in with you?"

I didn't really think about it that way. "Maybe we should ask Oppa if we can move in to the, um, house we cleaned out last week. He said it was for if our family got any bigger, and it has. You and Gregory and Hassan are family too."

Santanos stares at me like I hung the moon, and I never knew what that phrase meant until now. His love for me, for *me*, shines out of him so bright, and I can tell it's just for me even though I can't tell you why. I just know that all this love that's so bright it almost hurts to look at is just for me and he's so in love with me that he's never going to leave me or hurt me or make me feel anything but treasured. This amount of love is why we shouldn't be apart, because I'm looking at him the same way. I love my family, but Santanos is different. He's my person and I'm his, and that's it. That's all.

"Gregory, tell Hassan to organize the minions. We'll need them to pack up our bedroom at the mansion. We're moving in with the Foxilys," Santanos says, staring at me the whole time.

Gregory huffs like he's annoyed, but I feel him pinch my butt, so I know he's ok with moving in with me too.

"You should kiss me now," I tell Santanos. "You know you want to."

"Desperately," he whispers and pushes his mouth to mine.

He slides his tongue inside and we taste each other, and it doesn't feel as overwhelming as it did before. It's right. This is right. I need to spend a lot of time kissing Santanos, and giving him orgasms, and maybe sometime soon, I should think about an orgasm for myself too. I should maybe at least try it out even though sometimes it feels scary.

My grandma told me once that some of the best things in life are the scariest.

CHAPTER 16

𝓘 always thought it was a strange thing to say when my grandma said she was spitting mad. She never spat anything at all, but my papa does. I don't think he means to, but he's mad enough that he's trying to talk even though he can't, and he keeps shooting out spit and making clicking noises. He hasn't even used his phone to talk, but I can tell he's yelling.

Oppa and I don't really know what to do because Papa is just pacing all around the tables in the living room (one of them is missing), throwing up hands and not making any sense at all. I'm not too worried because his light hasn't gone out or anything. He's still pretty bright and full of love.

I was confused when he kidnapped me because he's so full of love and he didn't seem like the kind of person to just kidnap a gas station worker, but that turned out to be a mistake I made. Well, it was the best mistake I ever made, so I don't regret it.

"What is he doing?" Santanos asks, slipping his hand into mine as we watch Papa.

"He's just working out his feelings," I reply, trying not to let him know that my papa doesn't think he should move in with us.

"I can see that. He's aware that we can't read his lips right?"

"He knows," Oppa grunts. "I moved your bed and bedroom into the townhome next door. Romily thinks you'll be happier in your own space, and he thinks our place will be a bit too crowded with three extra people."

I wrap my arm around his shoulders and rest my cheek on his hair. "Thanks, Oppa. I think it would have been ok, but maybe a little crowded with the bathrooms in the morning."

Oppa grunts and leans a little into me, and his purplish light brightens up with his love for me. He has just as much love as Papa and Bellamy do, but it's just a little more colorful than mine. I thought it was gray at first, but I was wrong. It's like a really pale but kind of dark purple. It's hard to describe. I don't know why it's purple, but it is.

I like it. It matches Papa's golden light. They look very pretty together.

"Maybe you should hug him," I suggest when Papa bangs into the corner of a table and hurts his thigh.

Oppa moves fast, catching him before he can kick the table out of the way.

"Oppa doesn't like anyone moving his tables."

"Telling us that makes me want to rearrange the furniture," Gregory lets me know.

I pull him into a tight side hug. "It would be a good prank, but you should wait until they start liking you enough that they can laugh at a prank." I stop for a second, realizing, "Oppa would probably stab you with his sword if you moved his tables before he likes you."

"I would stab you many times," Oppa says, holding Papa in a bear hug.

Gregory looks like he's deciding if he wants to risk it, but Hassan comes up and helps me keep him out of trouble by standing on his other side.

Santanos lets go of my hand but grabs my wrist and stands in front of me, pulling my arm around him like a shield of protection. "While I do find it rather intriguing that you of all people delivered my mate to me, I find it ever so delightful that he's decided to bring me into his family rather than joining mine. But, Romily, I think I have news for you that you're going to absolutely love hearing, if you'll listen."

I'm surprised Santanos has news for my papa, and Hassan leans over and whispers, "A mate is like a husband or wife, but for demons it's more permanent than that and has a magical meaning too."

Oppa's head goes sideways as he looks at us. "Edovard is your mate?"

"It's the only explanation I can come up with for why he's able to feed me like he does," Santanos explains.

That riles Papa up again, and he starts fighting against Oppa's hug. Normally I would say that Oppa should let him go, but my papa looks like he wants to stab Santanos, and I think it's a good thing Oppa doesn't let him go this time.

"They are not fucking," Bellamy sighs from where he's sitting on the couch wiping down his biggest gun.

Papa's head whips around to look at Bellamy, and he points at him.

Bellamy rolls his eyes. "I already asked."

"But if Edovard ever wanted to fuck us, he knows he's welcome to. We're not going to hold him back from doing whatever the fuck he wants," Gregory announces loudly and grumpily.

I kiss his hair to thank him for standing up for me even though he doesn't need to. "I'm probably going to try it someday," I tell Papa as my stomach grumbles. "I really want to hear Santanos' news, and can we eat? It's been ages since we had dinner." This will be a second dinner, I guess, if I can get everyone on board for a meal. I hope I'm not the only one who's hungry. Oh, maybe that's why Papa's so mad. I bet he's hangry. I get that way too. "Should we order pizza?"

"That sounds lovely," Santanos replies, looking up at me.

Sometimes it just kind of makes it hard to breathe when he looks at me with his pretty blue eyes and loving smile. My heart pounds in my chest and my body gets warm all over. I love the way he makes me feel even though sometimes it's too big, but not this time. I'm safe at home and all my family is with me; it's the perfect time to let him take my breath away.

"Not even you can deny that look, Romily."

Oppa's words remind me that we're supposed to be planning dinner, so I just kiss Santanos really quickly and get back to the plan. "Can I try the kind that has the sauce on the top? I've never tried it before, but it looks like it could be good."

"Sure, pupper," Oppa agrees, pulling out his phone.

Papa huffs and crosses his arms and looks at Santanos like he still might try to stab him, but I can tell he's over the worst of his temper tantrum, so I let go of my—well, I don't know what to call them—and go to him, offering him a hug too.

"I know you're going to like them once you get to know them," I whisper when he lets me hug him.

He puffs air through his lips like pfft and rubs his face on my chest.

"Santanos is really nice. He's good at taking care of people, and he's so full of love for everyone. I know it's hard to believe, but he loves me so big that sometimes it hurts to look at him because he's so bright. You're going to like him when you give him a chance. He's my person, and I know my person is going to fit in with my family. I just know it."

Oppa squints at Papa and then says, "He's not convinced, but he's willing to let bygones be as long as Sant—no, Gregory, drinks some arsenic." He smacks Papa's butt and shakes his head. "They knew it wouldn't work, and I'm immune."

From behind me, I *feel* Gregory's anger.

"You cut Hassan's throat open! You weren't even in any danger."

<Bellamy: Please stop giving Fox credit for my work.

Gregory: I blame all of you, not just the person with blood on his hands.

Bellamy: But I really want this feather in my hat.

Hassan: Remind me if you've been beheaded yet?

Oppa: He hasn't.

Bellamy: I thought you were on my side!

Oppa: Right now I'm on the side Romily is standing on.

Papa: And I'm standing right next to Edovard.

Bellamy: This is going to suck.>

"Pizza!" I cry out, because feeling Gregory getting that angry is scary and weird, and I've got to stop them before something happens.

"Careful, Gregory," Santanos murmurs softly. "The ward around this place will kick you out if you get violent."

Gregory takes a deep breath and releases it. "I'm going to go oversee the minions."

"Are they here?" I ask, looking toward the front door.

"They will be," Gregory growls, heading toward the front door, and Hassan follows him, calling over his shoulder, "We'll order dinner."

I let go of Papa and grab Santanos' hand, pulling him to the living room and sitting with him on my lap. "Can we please hear what Santanos' news is now? Can we please stop fighting? Can you just… can't you just trust me? Santanos and Gregory and Hassan belong in our family. I know it. I can feel it inside. I don't like it when you fight. It's wrong. We should be a family. We have to be a family. It's the right thing to do."

I'm not sure where all those words are coming from, but they're true. I know they are. We have to be a family. We *have* to be.

Papa looks sad, and he comes over to me and Santanos scoots over and they both sit in my lap, and Papa pets me while Oppa sits down too, pointing at Papa to show me that he's talking for him. "Ok, pupper. We trust you. Santanos, Gregory, and Hassan are part of the family now. We will learn to love them."

"We will?" Bellamy asks. He's already finished playing with his gun, I guess.

Papa nods firmly. That means he's decided, and he's the one in charge of our family, so that means that everyone is going to love everyone else.

Relief slams into me like some of the guys at my old gym used to do when they were saying hello, and suddenly I'm very tired and hungry. I lean back against the sofa and rest my head, closing my eyes for just a second. "Tell us the news, Santanos," I sigh, happy to have all the fighting done.

Santanos pets my head while Papa moves over to Oppa. "I think our Edovard may be the reason the balance of good and evil is being restored so quickly."

"What?" That's Bellamy.

"What do you mean?" That's Oppa.

Papa just looks a little proud of me or himself or both, maybe? What's the word for when you're proud but also it's a little mean too? That's Papa right now.

<Papa: The word you're looking for is smug.
Me: Oh, thank you.>

Papa looks smug.

"Since Edovard joined my organization, the two percent that we've been struggling to fix for the last twenty years has jumped to one point two percent. This morning it was one point five. I can't prove the movement on the percentages is specifically because of him, but the correlation between what he convinces the minions to do and the jump in the percentages is too uncanny to ignore," Santanos explains to my family.

I don't know what some of those words mean, and I don't have time to look them up, but I guess someone will explain it to me later.

"What is he doing?" Bellamy asks, glancing from Santanos to me and back.

"He suggested a youth program for vulnerable kids and a recycling business is in the works because of his suggestion. He saved Saxon's employees from his son and picked your replacement. So far. The minions all adore him at least as much as I do, and he's spending most of his time just healing the random internal pains that my minions carry with them."

"Why would the minions start a recycling business? They don't do anything without an evil motivation. Is he turning your organization good?" Bellamy asks doubtfully.

"I would never. Being evil is very important to them. They're going to blackmail the businesses that use their paper recycling," I explain, a little offended that he thinks I would do that to Santanos. "They like being evil. It gives them joy. I wouldn't take that away from them."

"And how is it evil to create and maintain a youth program for vulnerable kids?" Bellamy challenges.

I take a deep breath, puffing out my chest to meet his challenge. "We're going to teach them life skills that will help them if they decide to become business people, like lockpicking and tax evasion. And we're using the charity so we don't have to pay the government taxes, too."

"And how does saving a bunch of restaurant employees help the cause of evil?" This time he doesn't sound like he can't believe I'd be helpful to Santanos' minions without stealing their joy.

"Well, actually, in that case, it was his Augur responsibilities that fixed a great evil," Santanos replies. "And Edovard, will you explain why you picked Gaanbatar?"

"Did he win?" I ask, surprised he already knows who killed that guy from the club.

Santanos nods and gives me a sweet kiss on the cheek. "He won within ten minutes of the challenge going out."

"Oh good. He's a good man. I like him a lot. I don't know if I can tell you why I picked him besides that he's full of light and love. He just felt like the right person, like he belongs with us, in our family. Maybe he won't want to be part of our family, but he belongs with us for sure."

Santanos gives me another sweet kiss. "That's a good enough reason for me, sweetie. I trust your instincts."

My heart just loves hearing that. "I like it when you say that to me. Not a lot of people trust me."

"People are basically the worst, so don't let them steal your confidence. You keep on being who you are, and I will keep on trusting you, and the world will become a better place for it," he tells me with another kiss.

"You two are worse than those two," Bellamy complains, waving his hand at Papa and Oppa, who are also cuddling with their hearts just thumping for each other. Their inner lights are shining bright together and pulsing with the same tempo. It's really pretty to see them together.

Papa's digital voice breaks the moment when he says, "It's weird that Santanos is encouraging Edovard to make the world a better place, right?"

<Papa: I stand by what I said.

Gregory: It's a strange hill to die on, but at least you're dead.>

"I exist to keep the scales balanced. Right now they are out of balance, so yes, it's strange that I am concerned about making the world a better place, but also not since it needs to be better," Santanos replies, scratching the back of my neck and making it really difficult to pay attention to the rest of the conversation.

Whatever they say, it's nothing compared to how good his fingernails feel against my scalp. The only thing keeping me awake is the pizza coming, and as soon as that's here, I'm taking my family next door for cuddles and sleep.

CHAPTER 17

Adding Gregory, Hassan, and Santanos to my bed was the best idea I've ever had. I let my love trickle out to those three, snuggled in with Santanos and Gregory right next to me on each side and Hassan tucked into Gregory's back. My love has been seeping into them for hours while they sleep. I slept for a while but woke up for no reason and have been enjoying the light show from my family. Something must've happened while we were all asleep because all three of them have tiny fireworks going off inside them. It's like my love is sparking with theirs and setting off little glittery explosions.

I wonder why it's happening, but not enough to do anything that might stop it. For no reason at all, I think it might be a fireworks show just for me, like maybe the magic that lets me see the love inside people is showing me how important my love is to this family. They loved each other before I ever met them, but they need me to help them remember how to love each other best.

I don't know a lot of things besides how to help people love each other, but I do know that this show is just for me, and I don't want to wake them up and accidentally stop it. It's too beautiful to spoil.

"Gina Theropolis, Nashville, Tennessee. She's killed a hundred old people already. You gotta stop her because she just killed someone's nona and they're so sad. They lost the most important person in their family." I wipe the tears away, sniffling at the vision that I got this time. "Two of her grandkids are going to die because she's dead. We need to save them. Their family is going to hate them to death. Please stop them."

I don't know if the depot has anyone to help the victims of the people spreading this much evil into the world, but those cousins shouldn't be even more victims. Their family is so evil, and the nona was the only thing keeping them from saying and doing bad things to the two kids who don't fit in. They're different like me, and I don't want them to give up hope because their family doesn't love them.

Santanos wipes the tears from my cheeks with a fancy hanky and Gregory gives me a hug with a sour expression while Hassan looks around at the people in the diner we're eating breakfast in like he's going to kill them if they do the wrong thing. I appreciate that he's scary and doing his thing to protect me, even though it's not really what I need right now. It's his way of loving me, and that's what's important. He's not actually hurting anyone.

"The depot doesn't do that, sweetie pie. They stop the evil and handle the contracts; they're in charge of a lot of things, but they don't help people like that," Santanos explains.

"That's not good enough. If we stop the person murdering nonas, that's fine, but there's more to stopping evil than just killing people. We need to help the victims. They're that word that means they're victims on the side of the crime. Like if a building gets blown up, but the point of blowing it up was to kill the guy on the top floor. What's the word for that?"

"Collateral damage," Hassan replies quickly.

"Exactly. There are people who are collateral damage and we need to help them," I beg Santanos.

Santanos kisses my forehead while he thinks about it. "You're going to have to ask the council to start an advocacy group for the victims of the victimizers. That's not going to go over well with the minions, you know. You might have a hard time convincing the council too. This kind of thing will need a unanimous vote, baby. You'll have to convince the evil representative on the council that this is in the best interest of evil too."

"I can do it. I will. I just might need some help." I start out that declaration pretty confident, but at the end I realize that I'm not going to be able to talk to the council without a lot of help. I'm really bad at speeches in front of people. I get nervous.

"I think if you convince some minions to help you, that would be the best way to start. You have my full support, my love, but this is going to have to come from you. My magic is telling me to let you take the lead on this," Santanos explains, holding my face between his hands. "If it's going to happen, you have to make it happen."

If that's what the magic is telling him, then that's what I'm going to do. So far the magic hasn't been wrong about things. People need to die, but I also think some people need to live. The council needs a part of it that helps some people live when they need to be alive.

"Can we take breakfast to the office, so I can start talking to the minions?" I'm still hungry, but there's an important time crunch on this. Those kids that need help need it tomorrow.

"Of course, baby."

Gregory waves our server over and demands boxes while Santanos pays for the food. In a few minutes, the four of us leave the diner, walking the short distance to the office. We enter the elevator together, but I get off before the other three, kissing them all for luck.

The floor I'm on is the "idea floor." There's a lot of projects that come out of this department, but the point of it is to get ideas and then tell the right department about it so they can make it happen. Hassan told me to find a minion here and tell them what I want to have happen, so I go up to the first group of minions I see.

They're shifters in their beast forms, and they are so cute. I've seen some really scary werewolf shows where the beast forms are terrifying, but that's not how it is in real life. Thankfully. These shifters are a mix of animals. There's two dogs, a cat, and a dragon. The dragon is the cutest one, but they are all pretty adorable.

There's lizard people that look like dragons, but real dragons are furry with huge eyes that make them look as cute as babies do with their big eyes. They have curly hair and floppy ears that they can make stand up on their heads like rabbits. They're so cute that sometimes I want to pet them. I can't because I'm not allowed to just pet people, but sometimes I wish I could. I'd really like to know what their long whiskers feel like. Grandma told me they were like a cat's whiskers, but they're so long and look like ribbons, so I don't think they're actually like a cat's.

"Hi. I'm Edovard Folange, Santanos' assistant," I announce, waving at them.

The dragon wiggles in excitement. Sometimes people just have to wiggle when they can't contain their emotions, and this person is definitely happy to meet me, which is good because I'm excited about maybe working with a dragon too. "Hi! I'm Zilong because of my purple hair. I heard you give really good hugs. Can I have one?" they chirp like a happy bird (I can't tell if shifters in their beast forms are boys or girls).

I open my arms wide enough for everyone. "All minions are welcome to come to me for hugs," I tell them, hugging the four of them all at once when they crowd in.

One of the dogs licks my cheek. "I'm Shilo, this is my mate Kyra, and this is our friend Aguirre."

"I'm glad I get to meet you. You all look very happy and healthy. Do you like your jobs?" All of them have the perfect amount of light inside them, and that makes me glad I found them first. It would be hard to get help from people I'm trying to heal; I'd probably get distracted.

Kyra also licks my other cheek, and the kitty rubs their face against mine, telling me, "We love working in R and D. It's always an adventure here. Do you like your job?"

"Oh, I really do!" I can't help squeezing them all a little tighter. "I love being here, and I really like all the minions I've met."

"Well, we are super loveable," Kyra giggles.

"Why are you in a puppy pile?" a deep and sad voice says from behind me.

We all look at another shifter person in their beast form. This one looks like a racoon, but like one of those drawings of fluffy racoons with red hair.

<Papa: You're thinking of red pandas. I think they're a kind of fox.

Oppa: They are the OG panda, named before the giant panda, and they're named that because they eat bamboo, but they're the only members of their family, Ailuridae.

Papa: Did you...did you just fact check me?

Oppa: https://nationalzoo.si.edu/animals/news/red-panda-bear-and-more-red-panda-facts>

I think he's even cuter than the dragon, except he's really sad. Plenty of light, it's just the sad color. I release the other shifters and open my arms to him. "Do you want to be in the middle? I'm Edovard, Santanos' assistant."

He sighs and steps into my arms and everyone surrounds him, putting him in the middle of the standing puppy pile. "I'm Bando. Why are you making puppy piles in R and D?"

"I need help, but there's always time for hugs, especially before asking for favors," I explain, which makes everyone cuddle in closer. Someone licks me again, and I wonder if I should tell them I'm not a tootsie pop.

"What do you need help with?" Zilong asks excitedly.

I blow out a breath and decide to just put everything out there and hope they'll want to help me. "I need to figure out how to make helping people evil enough that the evil council guy will approve my idea."

The minions all straighten up, looking at me with confusion. Bando is right in front of my face, and his huge golden eyes stare at me as he says, "Maybe you need to explain everything before we can decide if we can help you. Minions don't usually help people. We're usually busy doing bad things to them."

That's probably why Santanos said this would be a hard thing for the minions to accept, but the magic thinks I can do this, so I'm going to do my best.

"Sometimes evil people kill nonas, and when the nonas die, the people that they're protecting are left without any help at all. And maybe some of those people might do something with their lives that's important, but without their nonas protecting them, they end up dying before they can do the important thing that they could have done. They're collateral damage. Maybe the nona is evil and good kills her, so what happens to the people who she was protecting? Maybe they die, and that's good for good, but it's bad for evil, right? But it can also go the other way, where it's bad for good, but good for evil. It doesn't really matter. The problem is that good and evil are both just ignoring the collateral damage, and it's not right. We need—um—a group of people" —I can't remember what Santanos called it— "that help the people that aren't protected by the nonas anymore."

The group of shifters all stare at me with big, adorable eyes as they think about what I said.

"So you want to get council approval for an advocacy group for the people who are collateral damage when the council's organizations act, whether the act is good or evil. Is that correct?" Bando asks, never looking away from my eyes. I bet he's really good at the staring game.

"Yes. That's what Santanos called it," I confirm, relieved he understands what we need to make happen.

"And it would be neutral, not discriminating between the victims of good or the victims of evil?" Kyra asks with her thinking cap on.

Shilo licks me again. "I think we can probably put together a plan and a presentation, but it's going to be a hard sell. Evil just assumes that anything bad is good for evil."

"But it's not fair to those kids who are going to die if we don't help them," I insist. "There are kids in Nashville right now who are going to be told that they are evil and worthless and they are going to die because this lady killed their nona. Someone is going to go kill that lady, but that doesn't matter because the kids are still going to die because that lady killed their nona. We also need to get someone in Nashville to go save those kids because it's not fair that we do bad things and the other side does good things, and those kids die because of it. We have to save those kids."

My upset leaks out of me and my shifter minions scooch in really close and lick me on my cheeks, neck, and hands, trying to help me calm down. Someone wipes away the tears that escaped while I was talking, and Aguirre starts purring to help too.

"Ok, we can see how important this is," Shilo says, looking at his mate, who says, "I have a cousin in Nashville who I can send to get the kids. Is that ok? Do you have names and addresses? Anything. We're pretty good at finding people."

"I only know the murderer's name. Gina Theropolis. She killed the kids' nona and the depot is going to send someone to kill her."

Kyra licks me again and Bando snuffles my neck. Aguirre purrs harder, and Shilo says, "Ok, we will dispatch Kyra's cousin to track down the kids. If you know what they look like, that would be helpful too, but we can probably track them down with the name of the murderer."

"They're cute," I sniffle. "One has curly blue hair and looks like one of those goth kids that skateboards a lot. The other one is blond with hair down to their shoulders. They like to wear suits with bow ties, but they like fun prints instead of the suits that business people wear. They don't fit in with their family and it's hard to be themselves, but their nona made their parents behave, but now she's gone and they're going to have a really hard time."

"Don't worry, we'll find them," Bando promises me, "and we're going to make sure the entire council votes for your advocacy group because it's a good idea, no matter which side you're on."

"I'm really glad you're the minions I met first. Thank you all." I hope they know how important they are to me and the kids they're going to save. Santanos has the best minions. They're probably even better than my grand sugar daddy's minions.

<Romily: I hate that I agree.

Grand Sugar Daddy: Me too. Those fuckers are cuter than mine and far less prickly.

Romily: Think we can recruit them?

Santanos: Absolutely not.

Grand Sugar Daddy: Challenge accepted.>

CHAPTER 18

The council in charge of the world has ten people on it, and they are all pretty intimidating, but the middle person, Mx. Elliven, is the one that gave my Oppa permission to give my brother a coin—it was important at the time, but I was pretty distracted by a lot of things happening, so I don't really remember what the coin did. Anyway, Mx. Elliven is also in charge of my presentation to the council, so I'm supposed to stand in front of them and do my speech.

I'm really lucky that my shifter friends helped me memorize my lines when I told them that I wasn't a very good reader.

Before the meeting gets started, the door bangs open and my Oppa and Papa walk in. They're both silent, but it feels like their entrance is so loud that it echoes in the room. There's a big audience, almost as big as when I was here last, and they all shut up all of the sudden which makes the silence so much louder. Oppa shows me his phone to let me know that he's doing the same live stream that Papa did when it was Oppa's turn in here.

That makes me a little nervous, but I'm also pretty relieved they could make it. They were in Tennessee when the council told us to come. It would be hard to do this without them, even though I have

Santanos, Gregory, and Hassan with me. I wanted my whole family to be here. The only person missing is—

Bellamy jogs in and now everyone is here. Knowing they're here makes my nervousness less nervous.

"Edovard Folange is here to present the council with a new program opportunity," the announcer guy calls out, interrupting the quietness.

Mx. Elliven's stare feels like getting stabbed in chest with a long needle; it's pretty intense. "Mr. Folange, please proceed. We understand you want the council to approve a new aid program."

I take a deep breath and flick the pins and needles in my hands out—I think I might have been clenching my fists without knowing it. It doesn't stop me from shaking a lot while I talk. "Yes, Councilor Elliven. It's important to take care of the people who are victims of the people the magic kills. Sometimes my Oppa might kill a bad guy, but that bad guy killed someone's protector, and we should help the person that needed that protection. I'm an Augur. I see the bad things that the people who need to die do, but I also see the consequences of their actions."

I'm still shaking like a leaf and my voice is kind of wobbly, but I know what to say and I practiced hard, so I keep going as best as I can. This might be the scariest thing I've ever done, but it's also maybe the most important, so I have to keep going. "My Oppa killed an angel of death, and that angel of death killed the grandmother of two kids who would have died because losing their nona—um, grandmother—was the same as losing everyone in the world who loved and accepted them for who they are. My minions helped me save them, but the council needs an advocacy group that will be on call for those kinds of situations—"

One of the council guys, the evil one I was warned about, interrupts my speech. "You used the minions of evil to do good's work?"

The interruption throws me off, and it takes me a minute to remember what I'm supposed to do if I get interrupted, but Aguirre and Bando were really good at helping me with this, so I take a deep breath and answer. "I told Santanos' minions about the problem I was having, and while we were brainstorming ideas for this presentation, one of them asked their *good* cousin to help the kids from my vision. Just because we're evil doesn't mean that everyone in our family is evil. We don't know what those kids will grow up to do. They might grow up to be the most amazing art thieves on the planet, or they might grow up to work in a call center. We don't know, but just because we don't know doesn't mean we can't care. If we invest in the future, then when we get to the future, we will already have our rewards waiting for us, and that is true for both good and evil."

"You're telling us that the minions of evil helped you come up with a plan for an advocacy group for people affected by the contracts that the depot disperses to the Reapers?" one of the other council members asks in a downright rude tone. She's darker than the evil guy as far as the light of love goes, so I guess I don't have to be surprised that she's being mean.

"Of course they did. The minions are always up for a challenge and even helped me figure out how to make the advocacy group neutral so that everyone can see it's a good idea." I swallow hard and try to make them see how important this is. "I know that this needs to happen. I'm an Augur and I know things, and this is one of those things that I know. We need people who will help the people who need help no matter if they are good or evil. If their lives are going to go off course because of what we do, we need to fix it for them so that what we're doing isn't causing more harm than it needs to cause for both good and evil. Evil doesn't want to lose the ten percent of people it needs in order to maintain the balance, and good shouldn't want to lose any of the ninety percent of people it needs to maintain the balance. We need a neutral group to make sure that we are taking care of the future as best as we can."

Grandpa D gets everyone's attention when he leans forward, but his love is shining super bright, so I know whatever he's going to say, he loves me and is really proud of me right now, and seeing that really helps with the scaredy cats doing somersaults in my stomach. "I think you've done well convincing us of the importance, but you're the only Augur that has ever said anything about the collateral damage. You can't carry the weight of the advocates on your back, so how will they know who they need to help?"

I'm relieved that my minion friends knew they would ask this question because I didn't even think about it. "I talked to twenty seven other Augurs, and even though that's not very many of them, all of them said that they would report to the depot who needed help, if that was something the depot wanted them to do. Almost all of them that I talked to told me that when they first started, they tried to tell the depot who to help, but since the depot didn't have anyone to go out and help them, they stopped reporting that. I think that all the council's Augurs can identify the people who need help. If the council makes an advocacy group, the Augurs will be able to tell them where to go because the magic wants this to happen."

Mx. Elliven looks startled at those words. "Magic wants this?"

"Yes, it does. I feel it. I know it. The magic wants this really badly, Councilor."

"How would you know?" the mean one demands. "You're dumb as a box of rocks; how do we know you're even capable of interpreting what the magic wants and doesn't want?"

The silence in the room is even louder than when my Oppa and Papa walked in.

No one likes being called stupid, and I especially hate it because I'm not book smart at all, but I can't help the giggle that bursts out of me when that woman's eyes go buggy at the sight of my family suddenly standing between me and her. Three good, three evil, and me behind them, and each one of them is threatening her with a real bad time without even saying a word.

With the silence broken by my laugh, Grandpa D clears his throat. "Noe, you might want to apologize to our beloved Augur. His family isn't keen on people insulting him, as you might have noticed."

Before Noe can respond, the evil councilor bangs his hand on the table in front of him and laughs. "I vote for Edovard's idea, because fuck you Noe."

One of the other councilors immediately says, "I also vote for Edovard's idea for the same reason: fuck you Noe."

Mx. Elliven bangs the gavel. "Noe is disqualified from voting for being a moron; are any opposed to the founding and development of an advocacy group for the victims of our systems?"

The silence among the councilors is just as loud as when Noe insulted me.

<Papa: Took her life in her own hands, you mean.

Oppa: I wonder if the magic has her replacement picked out yet.

Papa: I'm sure we'll find out soon.>

I'm not sure what that means until Mx. Elliven bangs their gavel again. "The council approves the advocacy group. Santanos, please send your minions' plans to the council's secretary, as well as to Annette and Giuseppe. Thank you, Mr. Folange, for bringing this need to our attention."

I smile wide and bow because it feels right. "Thank you, Councilor Elliven, and the rest of the council except Noe." I give the woman a sad look. "I forgive you because I don't need unforgiveness messing with my heart, but my family isn't as nice as I am, and half of them are killers, so you should probably try to hide."

I don't even feel bad about telling her that, even though it means she's probably going to die soon. Some people just don't belong in this world anymore, and that's all I have to say about that.

Santanos steps up, stopping the council from leaving right away. "Excuse my interruption. I didn't want to interfere in this because I knew that my mate could handle this meeting, however, since he accomplished his goal without my interference, as I knew he would, I have a few words for you. Especially you, Noe van Dongen. Edovard Folange has, without purposeful intention, brought the balance that we all have been so diligently working to restore to just nine tenths of a percent in need of rebalancing. We are currently sitting at eighty nine point one percent good versus ten point nine percent evil, and I fully expect that once the depot gets his idea for an advocacy group up and running, that the balance will be fully restored. When that happens, please remit your heartfelt thanks to this man to my office. Edovard is mine, and I will be keeping him." He pauses for a moment and looks at the woman who insulted me. She looks really pale now. "Except for you, Miss Van Dongen, obviously."

He doesn't wait for the council to say anything; instead, he just grabs my hand and starts pulling me out of the room with our family following.

As soon as we get out the doors into the lobby of this floor, I let myself finally breathe again. My stomach rumbles now that the cats have finally gone away, and I feel really happy. A wiggle escapes, but what I really want is to celebrate with my family, so as soon as we get in the elevator, I hug Santanos tight and announce, "Let's have Kentucky Fried Chicken for dinner. We need to celebrate."

Everyone looks a little confused, except for my Papa who smiles at me the way he does when he likes my ideas.

Gregory's eyebrows come together as he says, "KFC is your idea of a celebration dinner?"

I shrug, too happy to be worried about anything else. "It's what my grandma used to get when my sister did something impressive like get straight As or win at debate club. I never got straight As or anything like that, so we never got to celebrate with KFC because of me, but I did something today, so I want to get my celebration dinner."

"If your grandparents weren't already dead, I would kill them myself," Gregory grumps then tells Oppa and Papa, "We're getting KFC to celebrate Edovard's accomplishment today, and then we're going to figure out how to kill a councilor. Everyone understand the plan?"

Papa's grin is wicked, Oppa nods once, and Bellamy just looks like he's already planning which gun he wants to use. Hassan kisses my neck, and Santanos squeezes me harder, and Gregory looks fit to be tied, whatever that means, but his inner light is pulsing with his love, and well, I'm pretty proud of that too.

"I'm glad you guys finally found something to help you get along," I tell everyone, and yeah, I know I'm the thing that brought them together, but I guess I might be a little evil too, because I'm ok with that.

CHAPTER 19

*C*elebrating with my family because of something I did is the best. No wonder my sister tried so hard to impress my grandma—I want to feel like this all the time. I know that's not going to happen and KFC would get boring if I had something to celebrate all the time, but once in a while it would be awesome.

While I'm going to town on the bucket of chicken that Gregory got for me, the rest of my family is talking about that mean councilor that called me dumb. They're planning on how to assassinate her, and since that was Bellamy's job before he became a—whatever it's called—

<Bellamy: My title is now Acolyte. I'm a Reaper-in-training. Not that I need the training.

Oppa: The training is to ensure you don't die at an inconvenient moment.

Bellamy: Every death is inconvenient.

Papa: But at least you can get over them now.

Bellamy: That doesn't make them less painful.

Oppa: I'm not sorry.

Papa: No one expects you to be. Tell your father thank you for saving your ass.

Bellamy: Thank you for saving my ass. Please stop killing me.

Oppa: I would like to blow you up just to make sure no one else can...

Bellamy: I hate that I have to agree to this.
Papa: There, there.>

Anyway, everyone has agreed to let Bellamy kill that councilor. I'm not sure if it's a good idea, but since she's lost all her love anyway, I only feel a little bad about it. Mostly I just feel loved. No one has ever loved me as much as these six people do.

When my stomach is full and my belly button feels like it's about to pop out, we pack up the rest of the food, and Santanos says, "Edovard and I need to make a trip to Hell to meet my parents. I would prefer to not give them any warning that we're coming. They likely saw the broadcast of today's meeting, and trust me, it will take them almost no time to show up unannounced if we don't head them off. I think we can all agree that we do not need Bacchus and Lilith making an appearance in the city."

"We'd have a problem getting them to go back," Gregory grumbles.

Santanos gives Gregory a smile, and his love for him brightens in a pulse of happiness. "Indeed. As it happens, it will be unlikely that we can get Edovard back home tonight. My parents will likely ensnare us somehow and make returning home a challenge."

Papa drops his jaw and widens his eyes, making him look like a shocked cartoon character.

Oppa just looks at us with his blank face. "He wants to know if you want us to come with you for protection."

That is not what I see on Papa's face, but Oppa and him have a psychic connection, so I'm probably wrong.

Papa closes his mouth and nods really fast.

Gregory looks at Hassan, and Hasson looks like he's thinking about it, and Santanos just smiles at them both.

Hassan decides to take Papa up on the offer—he doesn't say anything, but we can all see his decision on his face—and Gregory sighs. "Fine. You can come with us, but try not to kill Bacchus. Lilith gets bitchy when people try."

"Did you learn this the hard way?" Bellamy asks, almost laughing, but not quite letting it out.

Gregory makes a rude gesture with his hand, so I just grab it and pull him into a hug, picking him up so he can be close to my heart and soak up my love. "How do we get to Hell?" I ask, leading everyone outside—apparently Gregory isn't fit for polite company right now.

"There's a portal at the office; we'll just use that," Santanos replies, sneaking his hand through my arm and holding on tight.

Gregory finally relaxes when we get outside and takes a deep breath with his face in my neck. "You have too many muscles to be a good pillow," he complains, but I don't take it personally—he probably just needs a nap or butt pats or something.

Maybe he needs sex again. He said he gets grumpy without it, and I haven't seen him get any since…I don't remember. It's been a few days.

"Do we have time to get Gregory some sex first?" I whisper to Santanos—I don't think my dads would want me to ask that too loudly.

Gregory whines, but Santanos gives me a frowny face. "We probably don't have time for that. We can make it a priority when we get back."

"I really do not need to hear about your bedroom plans," Bellamy complains, hailing a taxi that stops and then another one that pulls up behind the first one.

"I tried to whisper." I don't think I need to apologize when I did what I could. Gregory's needs are important, and sometimes we have to talk about our needs and make plans for them.

Bellamy waves as he climbs into his taxi, and I put Gregory down so he can get in ours. Hassan takes the front seat and Santanos and Gregory sit in the back with me in the middle. The driver takes us to our work building, but it doesn't take long, so I'm not scrunched up for more than a couple of minutes.

When we all get out of the taxis, Santanos leads the way inside, Gregory looks up at me with those grumpy eyes while my dads and brother follow Santanos, so I pick him up again, and then us two and Hassan follow everyone inside.

"I'm really proud of you for telling me what you want, Gregory. It makes me really happy when you do that." I don't want him to stop telling me what he needs (even if he doesn't use words) because I'm not always smart enough to figure things out, and I need my family to tell me what they need and want from me so I can give it to them. "I like knowing what I can do for you."

He grumbles, but he's happy letting me carry him, so I just take that to mean that he'll keep on telling me when he wants my love and attention.

"It feels weird walking into the heart of the enemy," Papa's digital voice says as we're waiting for the elevator.

"Not as weird as it feels walking the enemy into the heart of our operations," Gregory snarks at him.

"We are not enemies," I remind them, because I guess they've forgotten since supper.

"We're family. Families don't always agree on every moral quandary, but we're lucky enough that we all have the same fundamental goals," Santanos replies in *that* voice. It's the one he used in the church in Rome —like he's trying to make anyone who hears it fall under his spell and love him. I like that voice a lot; he can use it with me anytime he wants.

Papa gives Santanos a dirty look while Oppa pulls him into a hug.

Bellamy sighs so loudly that I can hear it over the ding of the elevator. "It's ridiculous that I escaped Santanos' reach only to have my brother pull him close enough to put us all on the same side."

"You're just lucky we decided not to kill you after you slit Hassan's throat," Gregory tells him, popping up from my neck just long enough to say that.

"You're lucky I didn't kill him when he got in my way," Bellamy replies, so I decide to put Gregory in the corner of the elevator and Hassan helps by standing next to me and blocking the view so Gregory can't see Bellamy.

Honestly, they're bickering like siblings, so I'm not too worried about it. Brothers sometimes argue, and they're almost like brothers because Bellamy is my brother and Gregory is…well, I don't know, but not a brother. It would be weird for me to do sex with a brother. We're family though, so maybe they can be brothers and he can be my boyfriend or something.

Well, Santanos is my mate, and that's like being my husband, so I wonder…

I lean over to Hassan and whisper really quietly, "Am I allowed to have a mate and a boyfriend—well, two boyfriends?"

Hassan eyes me for a moment then slowly nods. "As long as Santanos thinks that's ok."

Oh, well I'm pretty sure Santanos wants that too, but I'll ask just in case. He loves Gregory and Hassan too, so I think it will be ok.

The elevator stops on the floor where the breakroom is, and we all get out, but I'm last since I'm in the corner, and when I finally get out, a bunch of my new minion friends are all hanging out watching a TV where the broadcast of my meeting with the council is being shown again.

Wow. I look really nervous and kinda fat.

As soon as the minions notice me, a cheer goes up, and they all start talking at once. Gregory puts his feet on the floor and I let him go, then he and Hassan start herding our family past the minions, getting out of the way so the minions can come talk to me. I'm glad they don't leave me behind, because I don't know where the portal is—though I bet the minions know.

"Hello, Minions! Did you see how good we did! We got the program approved!" I announce to them even though they already saw it. "We worked really hard and we won!"

The shifter minions that helped me start a big group hug with me in the middle, and it makes me happy to see them bright and shiny. I release a bunch of my love and let it soak through all of us. They don't need the boost, but everyone deserves love, and that's really why I'm here. Santanos needs my love, but so do all these guys too.

One by one, I kiss the tops of their heads, and some even get cheek kisses because they're sneaky. The dragon, Zilong, even manages to get lip kisses, which is adorable. Their little hairs on their face tickle me and make me laugh, which just sets off the joy of all my little minions friends. I'm so glad they decided to help me.

"Minions, we need to take the portal to Hell. Why don't you all plan a celebration for Edovard for tomorrow evening?" Santanos' love and affection for his minions shines out of him while he talks to them, and they all agree in a hurry, pushing me back to our leader.

I wave goodbye to them and then take up Santanos' hand and kiss the back of it because he just makes me so happy. "Thank you," I say for no reason except that I am just full of thanks about him.

"You're welcome, darling," he replies in that voice that I just love so much.

Papa grabs my other hand and squeezes it, giving me a happy smile while his love pulses brightly a couple of times.

I'm the luckiest I've ever been, and I know it. I've never been surrounded by people who love me this much. It takes my breath away.

We go into a room with three different portals on the wall, and Hassan stops in front of the one on the left. He motions to Oppa to join him, and Gregory grumpily points at Bellamy to join him behind Oppa and Hassan, leaving me and Santanos and Papa in the back.

Santanos whispers, "Protectors go first because we never know what we're going to find on the other side."

"I thought you protected Gregory and Hassan," Papa's phone says.

Gregory makes the same rude gesture without looking at us. He really needs some cuddles and sex as soon as we're done.

"We protect each other," Santanos replies, running a loving hand down Gregory's back.

Without any warning at all, Oppa and Hassan walk through the portal together, and then Gregory and Bellamy do, but Santanos waits for a few seconds before leading the three of us into it.

Walking through a portal isn't hard. It's just a little weird and makes me dizzy for a second because I was on carpet, but now I'm standing on gravel, and the room was bright, and here it's red. Red like—well, kinda like the blood that is pooling from the dead bodies all around us.

My dinner tries to come back up, but I manage to swallow it down. The blood and guts hide in the redness of the rocks and dirt, but I can still see the bodies with their intestines falling out.

"Ah, those are my brother's minions," Santanos explains. His eyes stop on a figure standing a little ways off, which helps me notice the person too.

They're bigger than me, and they're walking toward us, which makes them get bigger and bigger. "They're a giant," I whisper as Oppa, Hassan,

Bellamy, and Gregory all stand in a row with their swords ready. "I didn't even know Hassan and Gregory had swords," I whisper to Papa.

"They keep them hidden until they need them," Santanos murmurs, then calls out to the giant, "Ho! Brother! Are you here to die or escort us to the palace gates?"

The brother doesn't say anything, but a giant hammer just appears out of nowhere and he takes a swing at my family, scattering their line and hitting Hassan as he tries to roll away. He falls to the side, bleeding from his head, and his light just blinks out. The giant follows the swing of his hammer around and up—

It's going to smash Hassan!!

Something inside me just cracks like a huge boulder splitting down the middle, and angry fire fills me up, and then everything that's red turns as bright as the sun and as white as a new sheet of paper.

CHAPTER 20

"Where did you find it?" That's a new voice; kind of deep, but probably a woman.

"He's a person, not a thing." Santanos. He sounds the same way my grandma used to sound whenever I didn't understand my math homework even after we'd been working on it for hours.

"The last time someone insulted our pupper, we planned out their death in bloody detail. I'm sure you'll be hearing about an opening on the council in the next—what? Three days?" Gregory sounds grumpier than ever.

"Twenty four hours after we leave here." Bellamy probably won't take that long, but I think he's just giving himself some padding.

"Impressive." Hassan sounds good.

Hassan!

I bolt upright and jump to my feet, grabbing Hassan gently as soon as I see him. "You were hurt!" I have to make sure he's ok.

His love pulses as bright as anything even though his face stays blank, and he tips his head so I can see where he was hurt is ok now. "Dead, pupper. Gil killed me, but I'm ok now."

My eyes feel like they're going to bug out of my head. "How did you get ok from being dead? Are you like Oppa and Bellamy? Im-imm-imsomething."

"Immortal? No." He stops abruptly and looks at the only woman here. She's also a giant with dark red hair—the same red as blood—with fangs that poke out from her mouth and big black eyes. "I'm not immortal now, am I?"

The woman's eyebrow rises up in an incredible arch. "You currently have my son's life inside you—what do you think? That was a straight exchange, and if I had the power to do it, I would exchange it back, because my son is far more valuable to me than a disgusting ant like you."

"Ok. I'm getting really tired of people attacking my boyfriends, my mate, and my family. If you can't say anything nice, you don't get to say anything at all!" I don't think I've ever been this angry. It's a new feeling for me, but I'm just done with all this, this, *baloney!*

<Papa: ...

Oppa: ...

Bellamy: It's ok to say—

Papa: NO!

Santanos: NO!

Gregory: Don't you dare!

Bellamy: This is pure baloney.>

"Mother, meet Edovard Folange, my mate. Edovard, this is Lilith, a queen of Hell," Santanos says before his mom can call me out for being rude.

But really, she started it, and this whole trip has been so disappointing. Why did we want to introduce me to his parents if they're going to treat us badly?

Lilith narrows her dark eyes at me. "I suppose it makes sense you would latch on to the first succubat you meet," she says to Santanos.

Santanos suddenly steps directly in front of me, then Gregory and Hassan are right there with him. Papa literally climbs up me and sits on my shoulders, and Oppa and Bellamy move in front of Santanos, Hassan, and Gregory.

I wonder what the succuthingy is.

Santanos reaches back and grabs my shirt but talks to his mom, so I guess I'll find out what the thing is after this. "I didn't realize Edovard was a succubat. I would not have brought him here if I'd known that. We're leaving now."

Lilith rolls her eyes and huffs, putting her hand on her generous hip (my grandmother said she had generous hips too—I think it just means they're wide). "I'm not going to hurt your little pet. He's safe here."

Santanos pushes me backwards as he takes a step back too. "None of us are naive enough to believe you, Mother."

Not even me, and I'm used to people thinking I'm too dumb to know when someone's not a safe person (obviously, I can tell by their insides, but most people don't even believe I can see what I do).

"IS THAT A SUCCUBAT?" That loud question comes from behind me.

I spin to find a goat person with adorable nubby horns on his head and scary demon eyes. I probably shouldn't be afraid of how he looks, but goat eyes are super creepy, aren't they?

Oh, and he has a really, really big erection (I remembered the word!).

He rubs his penis, staring at me as he walks toward me.

"Back off!" Santanos barks, jumping in front of me again.

The goat man smiles widely. "Son! Did you bring me a sacrifice? What boon can I grant you in return?"

"I will literally kill you if you take another step toward my mate," Santanos growls.

It's probably wrong of me that I think his growl is adorable. He's just so pretty, and all those blond curls don't help him look tough. Not that looks matter, because he's probably way tougher than me, and remember I look like a big bodybuilder. I mean, I am that, so I look like I'm supposed to, but people get intimidated even though I'm really nice.

Santanos' dad stops walking while the rest of my family kind of shuffles so that half of them are in front of me and half are behind me. I'm starting to think I might be in danger. "Am I the succubat thing?" I whisper to Papa, who is still sitting on my shoulders.

He holds his phone in front of me and types with his thumb: *Yes.*

Oh. Ok. We should probably leave then.

"Where did you even find one?" Santanos' dad says.

Oppa suddenly growls and steps away from the circle, facing Santanos' dad. "We found him; that's all you get to know. My family and I are leaving now. You are going to go stand next to your wife while we leave. If that's too much of a chore for you, Bacchus, I have a question for you."

Bacchus' smile scares me when he looks at my oppa. "What's the question, Mr. Fox?"

"How many times have you been eviscerated by the talons of a thunderbird?" Oppa asks, pushing the group of us back toward the portal, which looks a little further away than I expected.

Plus there's a bunch of bodies on the ground looking like speed bumps. Someone's going to trip, and it's probably going to be me.

Bacchus' goat eyes squint at Oppa, but instead of answering the question, he just moves over to Lilith, so I guess he's probably already flown with a thunderbird, and I don't blame him for not wanting to do it again. It's really hard to fly with Oppa.

<Hassan: He wasn't talking about flying, pupper. He was talking about using his thunderbird feet to pull out Bacchus' guts.

Me: Oh. Thanks for telling me.>

"How attached to your parents are you?" Oppa asks loudly.

"Kill them if you must, Fox. I would miss Edovard more," Santanos replies just as loudly, but his light dims—not a lot, but even a little isn't good.

"*Now that is queer audacity,*" Papa's digital voice says even louder than the others.

Gregory laughs and we all can't help but look at our grumpy boy. He immediately scowls at us. "That was funny. I'm allowed to laugh."

"It was funny," I encourage him—not everyone has the same sense of humor, so it's ok if he thinks something is funny even if I don't.

He looks everyone else in the eyes, and then like they're all psychic, they turn to look at Bacchus and Lilith again.

"Mother, Father, please don't force us to kill you. Maybe we'll see each other again in another few years, but don't come looking for us. We will defend our Edovard with extreme prejudice." Even though I don't always know what he says, I love how Santanos talks so politely even when he's probably talking about killing his parents. It's nice that the Avatar of Evil can be polite even when he's threatening people.

Bacchus and Lilith both look at me like they want to eat me, and since I'm food for their son, I guess they probably do want to eat me. Fortunately, they don't try to do that, and our group makes steady progress toward the portal.

Lilith looks like my grandmother used to whenever she got my grades; it makes me feel yucky because Santanos doesn't deserve for anyone to look at him like that. "While I am very disappointed in you, I won't stand in the way of your happiness. Maybe with him you'll be able to finally claim the Earth in the name of demonkind. We let you become the Avatar of Evil with the hope that you would succeed where your brothers have failed."

"Your mother's right, son. We expected to be informed of your triumph over good by now," Bacchus adds.

"It's like you deliberately ignore my actual job description," Santanos wonders, and Gregory grunts.

"What are you talking about? You are the Avatar of Evil; what is so hard to understand?" Lilith demands, getting louder as we get further away.

"Body," Bellamy says and everyone pauses to quickly look down before we trip.

"As I have explained multiple times, Mother, I am meant to keep the balance. I'm not actively trying to take over the world. I'm just spreading enough evil to keep everyone on their toes." While Santanos explains that, I get over the body without tripping, but I slip on the intestines.

Fortunately Santanos is stronger than he looks, and between him and Gregory, I don't fall. I'm glad Papa knows how to hang on. He's really good at shoulder rides.

<Papa: Thank you, pupper. I really haven't gotten enough practice riding anyone, but it's nice to know I would succeed if I ever get the chance.

Oppa: ...

Bellamy: I feel like this should be a conversation in your own private chat.

Papa: Don't be ridiculous. We're talking about *shoulder* rides.>

"That's ridiculous. Why would you become the Avatar of Evil if you're not going to take over the Earth?" Lilith questions.

Bacchus is only about half as tall as her, but he puts his arm around her waist. "Son, why would you stay the Avatar of Evil if you can't take over the planet for all demonkind?"

Santanos sighs. "I'll put in my two weeks notice the next time I see my boss."

Lilith and Bacchus both smile and their happiness pulses, but even I can tell he's lying.

I don't say anything because obviously he's saying a little white lie so that we can escape faster, but a mean smile creeps up on my lips. I think maybe I'm getting a little more evil, but it feels good to not be the dumbest person in the room.

Bellamy warns us about four more bodies while Santanos and his parents talk over the gap between us. Eventually we make it back to the portal, and then we shuffle through it, and as soon as we're all back on the safe side, Hassan slaps the portal and it just disappears like it was never there.

When it's gone, he slaps the other two portals as well, and they also disappear.

Once they're gone, Santanos steps in front of us all, and for the first time since I've met him, he looks worried and a little sick. His insides are tumbling and shaking a little and the light of his love looks a little green like people get when they're about to puke.

"Ok, it's time to make sure no one ever finds out that Edovard is a succubat," he whispers. "This information cannot leave this room. My parents won't tell anyone what he is because they're not willing to share. However, if they mysteriously ended up permanently dead, I wouldn't pursue that investigation very hard."

"I think perhaps it would benefit the rest of us to understand what the hell a succubat is. I thought succubae were made up by humans," Bellamy says quietly.

"So did I," Oppa adds, which startles Papa as he's climbing back down off my shoulders (the ceiling isn't high enough for him to stay on my shoulders).

"Once upon a time when Lilith was courting Bacchus, she traded a favor with one of her old friends, Bona Dea. Bona Dea took some of Lilith's eggs and fertilized them with her—sperm, for lack of a better word. There were five eggs, and they hatched the first succubats. They were literally born to die. The only thing my parents ever said about them was that they were delicious and a single succubat could sustain their appetites for about four months before they were completely consumed. By the time Lilith and Bacchus started spawning the incubacchus, all of the succubats were dead. At least that's what they told us. Clearly at least one escaped."

<Papa: I've been thinking about this. We don't know who Edovard's line comes from, but has anyone checked on the sister? Is she also a succubat?

Santanos: I had a minion check in on her. She was aware of her own ancestry, but told us that the magic is only passed down to one child of a succubat in every generation. If she has a child, it will be a succubat, but she is not one.

Papa: We better make sure no one finds out about her.

Hassan: I have a plan.

Bellamy: Does it include murder?

Hassan: I don't plan to kill anyone.

Gregory: We have a new assassin for those kinds of jobs.>

No one knows what to say when he finishes explaining, and the quiet is one of those loud silences again. I get it, and I don't really know what to say either.

It makes me sick to my stomach that Santanos' parents made people like me just so they could eat them. That's the worst thing I've ever heard about, I think. Well, I guess there's a lot of bad things out there, and they are all as bad as each other. This bad thing belongs in that category. The category where Oppa kills people for being in it.

Oppa's hand creaks the leather on the handle of his sword, and that noise breaks the silence.

Gregory pushes his shoulder against my arm and growls. "I think it's about time the mansion gets a little renovation. I'm sure the minions that work there will enjoy a vacation to Jamaica for a few days."

Hassan's neck cracks when he flexes it. "I can make sure all the locks are engaged when they leave. It would be a shame if someone slipped in and found out about the illegal portals in the basement."

Bellamy and Papa grin widely as Oppa says, "It's strange how our vacation time is going to coincide with your renovations."

Santanos' smile is just as wicked as the ones on Bellamy and Papa's faces. "Strange indeed. Good thing you couldn't possibly know that my parents aren't immortal. They do love to pretend though."

Hassan gives him a less blank than usual look. "She lied about my immortality?"

"She's Hell's most notorious liar," Santanos giggles, patting Hassan.

Hassan puts his real blank face back on. "The dead are notoriously honest."

Santanos giggles again. "True."

CHAPTER 21

I don't really pay attention to everyone else on the way home. Instead of sitting in the back with my family, I sit up front with the cabbie because I have a lot to think about.

First, I'm not really sure what to think about my family killing Santanos' parents because of me. Yes, what they did was so bad it makes my heart hurt, and they would do that kind of thing to me if they could, so they haven't become better people since they killed all the people like me before Santanos was born. But how does Santanos feel about that? I never even met my parents and I couldn't plan their murder. That would make me feel very sad and probably angry too.

Speaking about being angry, I guess I accidentally killed someone today when he killed Hassan. My magic traded Gil's life for Hassan's death and that's confusing for me. I'm glad Hassan is alive, but it's kind of scary, isn't it? I don't know how I feel about murdering someone, but when you think about it, I tell the depot who the magic wants the Reapers to kill, so I'm the first step in the process of killing people. I guess the first person I killed was that guy in Milwaukee. I didn't actually do the murdering, but he would have kept on living if I hadn't said anything about him.

So I guess I'm a murderer now.

It's weird that I only feel a little bad about that. I should feel worse about being a murderer, right? Well, maybe I will later. Right now, I feel a little bad about it, but mostly I'm just happy Hassan is alive.

He's one of my boyfriends, so at least that feels right.

I have two boyfriends and a mate now. I didn't ever even think about having one special person and now I have three. That's pretty exciting. My life is always going to be full of love because of my family. I think it's probably about time that I just do sex too. Santanos will like that. Gregory too, probably. He needs sex, and I think he's probably healed enough that Santanos can take a little from him if everyone wants that. They said it feels good when Santanos feeds during sex, and I want everyone to feel good.

I turn to tell Santanos that he can feed from everyone a little bit when we get home, but it turns out we're already here, so I just decide to tell them when we get inside.

Papa, Oppa, and Bellamy are already here, and they stop before going into their front door to give me a big hug. I tell them that I love them and hug them back. Bellamy tells us to come over for breakfast, so that's good that we have plans for food since my side of the house doesn't have any food yet, I think. We've only just moved in, and we've been really busy so we're still figuring out all the things that we have to do to make it a good place to live.

Fortunately, my family has been living together for a long time already, so they know everything they need to be happy, and they like the really big bed that I bought for our bedroom.

"Pupper." Hassan gets my attention, jerking his head toward our front door, so I follow him and the others inside.

Santanos gives me a look like he's worried about me after I close the front door. "Want to talk about it, sweetie?"

Well, I guess I was thinking a lot on the way over, so maybe he's right to be a little worried. "I'm ok. I was just sorting through some of the stuff that's happened." I shrug, not really sure what to say about most of it, so I just focus on the one thing I'm sure about. "Gregory needs sex, so we should do that."

"Yes! That!" Gregory suddenly yells. "I need orgasms."

THE TROUBLE WITH TRYING TO LOVE A HELLION

I laugh, pulling him into a tight hug for just a second before giving him to Hassan. "And I think it would be ok for you to eat us while we're —um—sexing. The love inside of all of us looks really good and if you only eat a little, it should be ok. I can feed you the most though. Only take a little bit from Gregory and Hassan and only if they want you to. You have to have permission, remember?"

"Permission granted. Please eat me," Gregory says, just bursting with so much excitement that it gets me excited too.

"Me too," Hassan says less excitedly, but he's pulsing bright and happy with his love, so he's happy that Santanos gets to eat him too.

Santanos giggles and grabs my hands in his, looking up at me. His beauty makes it hard to breathe when he smiles up at me like this. "Sweetie, do you want to have sex with us too? Or do you want to do it like we did it before with Hassan and Gregory playing together while you and I play separately."

I didn't really think about that, but before I can Gregory is right there next to Santanos looking up at me too. "You can do whatever makes you feel good, and you don't have to do anything that makes you feel uncomfortable. Remember that your consent is just as important as mine and Hassan's and Santanos' too."

"Right. We all have to agree," I remember. "I wanted to try sex too. I think I'm ready."

"It's also ok if you decide you're not ready later. If you say stop, we will stop," Hassan adds.

Gregory snorts. "We're evil, not fucking barbarians."

Santanos' love almost blinds me in response to our—wait…

"Santanos, we didn't talk about it, but is it ok if Gregory and Hassan are my boyfriends too? Well, both of our boyfriends?"

Hassan said Santanos has to agree.

"Of course, sweetie. I've been with them for a very long time; I am happy to call them boyfriends instead of bodyguards," Santanos answers and the big pulse of happy love from both Gregory and Hassan is so beautiful that I have to blink back tears.

I pull them all into a big hug, happy because I've found my forever people. "Ok, good. I'm really happy about that and so are Hassan and

Gregory. We're a good family, so we should probably try sex together, don't you think?"

"Excellent. I haven't had a foursome in ages." Gregory sounds a little like an evil professor or like that cartoon mouse that was always trying to take over the world.

<Papa: Cartoon mouse?

Oppa: It's from a show called Animaniacs. It ran in the nineties.

Papa: How does Edovard know about a show that ran in the nineties? He was a toddler in the nineties.

Bellamy: I think you're focusing on the wrong thing here...

Papa: What are you worried about now?

Bellamy: Just the fact that you're fixing to read about your son getting it on with his partners.

Papa: I—I will not be kink shamed by you nor anyone.

Oppa: I'm going to go work out now.

Bellamy: Good idea.>

Santanos pulls me down and gives me a soft little kiss, then he turns and leads us all to the master bedroom. Once inside, he just starts taking off all his clothes, and Gregory and Hassan do too, so I guess it's naked time.

I don't usually get naked except when I'm showering, so it feels weird to take off my clothes, but then after I pull my shirt off, all three of my men stop and look at me. They look hungry too, but their insides are full of light and love, and I know they're not going to hurt me.

I'm not afraid, so I just open up my heart and let my love out while I unbutton my pants and push them off. I guess being naked with them isn't as hard as I thought it would be. Well, one part gets hard when Santanos starts pulling my love into his body. The tingles start and instead of worrying about it or getting scared, I just let it happen. All the practice I've gotten since we started hanging out all the time makes it easier to let my body react, and pretty soon, I have an erection just like all three of them do. I'm glad none of us are broken, but I feel kind of stupid for thinking Gregory's penis was broken that first morning we spent together.

"I don't know what to do," I tell them since they're all just standing there looking at me.

Santanos blinks and nods and takes one step forward, but then stops. "Mmm."

Gregory looks at him like he's gone crazy and shakes his head. "Edovard, why don't you go lay down on the bed. I think for the first time you should let us do the work."

"I can still watch, though, right? Because I learn better when I can see," I whisper—I know that I'm going to have to learn how to sex right.

"Of course, pupper. Go recline leaning against the headboard. You'll be able to watch and learn like that," he assures me, lifting his hand like he's going to touch me, but stopping. "We all want to touch and kiss and lick you all over, including your cock and ass; is that going to be ok? You can always tell us if you don't like something."

I think about that as I go over to the bed and lean back against the headboard in the center. The middle of the bed is my part of it, so I hope I'm where he wants me to be. "I'll tell you if I don't like something, and thank you for asking. Is it ok if I do that stuff too?"

"Hassan won't—" Gregory stops himself and looks over at Hassan with wide eyes. "Well, unless you want to bottom with him too."

Hassan looks at my erection for a second and I can't tell what he's thinking, but then he sort of smiles. "Maybe another time."

Gregory nods as Hassan picks Santanos up and brings him to the bed with me. "Hassan probably won't want us to play with his ass, but you can touch him everywhere else."

As soon as Hassan puts Santanos on the bed, my mate crawls over to me and sits on my abs, leaning down and kissing me. Oh, this kiss is tingly. He pulls love out of me and I split myself wide open to him to feed him as much as he wants. All of the sudden all three of my partners groan. Gregory lays down next to me and starts kissing my neck, and Hassan straddles my legs behind Santanos and his erection slides over mine, and oh my gosh! That feels so good!

The air whooshes into me and then makes a fast escape. I didn't know it could feel so good! No, I kind of knew, but no one has ever touched me like that! Santanos pulls from me again and everyone,

JENNIFER CODY

including me, makes a noise. We can't help it. It feels so good to be together like this, to be touching like this.

I reach for Gregory at the same time that I push my hand between me and Santanos, and I get both of their erections in my hands at the same time. They both fit perfectly in my big hands, and their happy noises nearly blind me when their light and love pulses brightly because of my touch. I don't know what comes over me, but something inside me suddenly needs to—well, it's like I need to kind of crush them so that they know how much I love them. It feels like a violent emotion, but I don't actually want to hurt them; I just want them to really, *really* feel my love for them.

So, I bite Santanos and grab Gregory's hip hard enough to leave bruises on him. Just little ones. As soon as I do, I pull back from them both, a little afraid they're going to get mad, but Santanos looks like he's in heaven with that look he got before—the one I love seeing because I know it means I'm doing something right.

Since I pulled back from Santanos, Hassan pulls him up and bites him on the neck right where I just bit him, and for a second, I feel really proud of him, and then Gregory is right in my face and his mouth crashes against mine, and I have to kiss him too. I need to. That feeling gets big again and that evil part of me that is ok with sometimes being a murderer reaches out and just tugs at Gregory's love. He groans as I push my love into him and pull his out, and somehow I feed it to Santanos too, and when I figure out how to do that, how to keep my boyfriend and mate connected and healthy and happy, I do the same thing to Hassan, pulling his love into me, pushing mine into him, and feeding all of our love to Santanos.

Suddenly they all freeze and I think I might have messed up, but then Gregory shoots up, he jerks on his erection, and three streams of white stuff splat all over my chest from him. Santanos' erection pulses in my hand and he also shoots the white stuff, and Hassan rubs himself against my little guy and he also, um, comes all over my chest too.

Oh wow. That's amazing.

"Did I do that?" I whisper, reaching out to touch each of their erections.

No one answers until they're all done twitching, but that's ok because I can't look away from the expressions on their faces, from the way our love swirls together and shines; it goes into Santanos, but then slips free too and lights Gregory up, then Hassan, and it even takes a little tumble inside me before going back to Santanos. It's like all that love that I've fed him gets bigger inside him; it becomes enough to share, and I don't know if he's doing it on purpose, but he shares it with all of us.

I can't look away. I don't want to.

"I think that was the way our magics are supposed to interact, my love," Santanos finally says. "I'm going to ride your cock, baby. I'm going to make you feel as good as you made us feel."

I don't really know what that means, but then Hassan's hand grabs my erection and he holds it up, and Santanos sits on it, pushing it inside his butt.

Wow. My mouth drops open and it's hard to breathe. My balls tingle, and there's a feeling at the base of my spine that feels like it's the start of something really big.

Gregory leans over Santanos' lap when he sits on my thighs, and he just sucks up Santanos' penis into his mouth. Santanos' hips jerk forward, which makes him slide over my, um, cock—that's a weird word—and all three of us make those moaning-groaning noises that we can't help making when things feel so good.

Hassan moves to behind Gregory and puts his cock inside Gregory's butt. Then things get really big really quickly. Santanos keeps on moving his hips and pushing his erection into Gregory's mouth and mine into the most perfect butt in all the world (now I know why it's the most perfect one ever), and Hassan does the same with Gregory, and the love that's been swirling around us gets bigger and bigger and brighter until it's hard to look at it because it's so, so beautiful.

Just as I close my eyes, all the tingles and good feelings explode inside me, and my entire body locks up as pleasure so great and strong that it almost hurts takes over my entire body. Just about the time it becomes too much for me to handle, it gets better, less big, more soft, and my body melts like I've just had the most relaxing massage and nap ever.

Wow.

"We need to do that every day," I decide as soon as my tongue starts working again.

Somehow we ended up in a puppy pile. I bet Bando would be so jealous of us right now.

That thought makes me giggle.

CHAPTER 22

Bellamy is really good at killing people. Maybe as good as our oppa. The councilor that told everyone that I was as dumb as a box of rocks loses a hand when she reaches for her gun, then he leans over her and stabs her in the stomach. I'm watching from across the street, so I don't know what he tells her, but whatever it is must be very scary because she doesn't know what to tell him and she opens her mouth and closes it a couple of times before she goes white as a sheet.

Darcy, the guy that helped us find Bellamy when he was kidnapped, stands next to me with a grin that's more wicked than even Santanos' is sometimes. He's the one that helped Bellamy get past the ward that all the councilors have. He said magic is about balance, so he just had to find the right balance to help Bellamy get past the ward.

I'm really glad he's on our side.

"After this we're going to kill Lilith and Bacchus?" Darcy asks Oppa. "Who's babysitting the pup?"

"Our puppers is mated to the Avatar of Evil. He doesn't need a babysitter. He has partners," Papa's phone tells him.

Darcy looks like a k-pop star, but those guys always look nice and Darcy looks dangerous. He scared me when I first met him, but I'm not too scared anymore. "Does that mean that we aren't going to kill him too?"

"No, we are family! We don't kill the people in our family." I turn to Oppa. "Darcy's part of our family, right?"

"I most certainly am not!"

"He is. He made a blood bond with both Papa and Bellamy, so he definitely is a part of the family. Like a distant cousin no one likes," Oppa explains, eyeing Darcy.

Darcy gives him an evil eye. "As long as I'm not expected to move into the crazy house. There's no version of reality in which I share a roof with the fucking Avatar of Evil and his cocksucking groupies."

I crouch down in front of him since he's so short. "Hey, let's be nicer to my mate and boyfriends, ok? We're friends, right? Plus you're part of my family and I love you. Do you want a hug? Sometimes we just need hugs to make us feel like we're part of our families, right?"

He stares at me like he isn't sure what to say, and his love inside is pretty dark, but I think that's because he doesn't want to let himself be loved. It's ok; I can help with that if he wants me to. It's not hard to help people when I'm so full of love because I have so much extra from my family. We have enough to share with him.

"No thank you, pupper," he decides, stepping back.

"Maybe next time. I'll ask next time, if that's ok? I'm really good at loving people." Someday he's going to want to be loved; I can wait for that day.

"You can ask, but don't get butthurt when I keep telling you no," he snorts.

I smile because I know grumpy guts when I see them. "I won't be. I can wait for you to be ready."

Bellamy jogs up to us with a naughty smile on his face. "How's that for up close and personal?"

Oppa pats his head. "Good job, son."

Bellamy rolls his eyes, but his huff of laughter tells us all he's happy to make our oppa proud.

Santanos pulls me down by my tie and kisses me hard. "Ok, my love, time to go to work."

I hug my family, except Darcy, and then me, my mate, and our boyfriends get into a taxi and head to the office. We need something called plausible deniability for what happens next.

I don't know what that is, but I know I love my family. The family that chose me and the ones I got to choose too. I am the luckiest person ever.

And they all lived happily ever after. (I always wanted to say that.)

THE END

<Santanos: Well done, my love. We have a gift for you.

Me: What is it?

shuffling

Gregory: Voila.

Me: Is that all the cushions for my nest? How did you get them?

Hassan: Gaanbatar picked them up for us while he was there.

Santanos: He also brought some of the decorations from your old room, and a chest full of blankets and quilts that it looks like your grandma made.

creaking noise

Me: My grandpa made these, and my grandma made this, and look! I helped with this one when I was eight!>

AUTHOR'S NOTE

Dear Reader,

Thank you for reading this book! I hope you enjoyed Edovard's adventure in saving the world. It's always the quiet ones that are the most dangerous, isn't it? Ok, and yes he was a bucketful of sweet summer child and adorable pupper.

What's next? Well, Romily's trouble with Fox and getting engaged will begin where this one leaves off with a sojourn to Hell to take care of some dangerous parents. Santanos is first generation incubaccha, so he's not going to be upset about whatever the Foxilys end up doing in Hell. It might be time for a new queen of Hell; I don't know. I'm a pantser; I will find out what happens when I write it.

If you enjoyed this book, please leave it a rating and a review! Join my newsletter to get access to all the free books that I have available, including "Fox Recruits a Mute Boy." I add freebies a few times a year, so there's always something new to look forward to. I've been cogitating a New Year's Eve party with the minions that includes evil New Year's resolutions. So far I've come up with always telling people to have the day they deserve when you're saying goodbye. Good? Evil? Neither? Have the day you deserve, ma'am. *snicker*

Have a suggestion for a mildly infuriating New Year's resolution?

AUTHOR'S NOTE

Email me at jennifercodymm@gmail.com. I will credit you for your contribution if I use your idea, probably by naming the minion who proposes it after you, so include a name you wouldn't mind for a minion.

Thank you for your support, love, encouraging words, and title ideas for book 4 of Murder Sprees and Mute Decrees. So far the runners up for the title is: The Trouble with Trying to Put a Ring on It, The Trouble with Trying to Plight One's Troth, and The Trouble with Trying to Hook a Harbinger.

I'm leaning toward the last one because it fits thematically and the consonance makes my brain bubbly.

For the love of MM,

Jennifer Cody

ABOUT THE AUTHOR

Jennifer Cody writes gay romance of a variety of sub-genres, though her favorite is paranormal romance/urban fantasy. She uses her husband's vast knowledge of all things man and mechanical to help her write, but takes literary license with her characters because they're romantic heroes, thereby making him shake his head in disbelief almost as often as she causes his incredulous laughter.

With three kids at home, the only time she has for boredom is 5 a.m. when everyone else is still asleep, and coffee usually keeps that at bay. When she reads, she usually binges an author's entire backlist for a few days but has a few one-click favorites she stalks. Her go-to sub-genres are gay PNR (Paranormal Romance) and UF (Urban Fantasy), but she has a soft spot for certain contemporary MM tropes (falling in love with the Manny, and small-town/rural stories).

Join Jennifer's Facebook group, Jennifer Cody's Cocky Cuties, for all kinds of fun shenanigans, live writes, schedule updates and more!

Sign up for my newsletter on my website to get more news and occasional serial shorts.

ALSO BY JENNIFER CODY

DIVINER'S GAME TRILOGY

Bishop to Knight One

Knight to Castle Two

Queen to King Three

DG Short Stories

(Only available on my website. Sign up for my newsletter to get these.)

Loki Adopts a Cat

The D'Aquinos Go to War

SHATTERED PAWNS SERIES

Spinoff of Diviner's Game

Pass

Capture

Promote

Shah Mat

Houston Hub Shorts

Forgotten Fox

Mr. Monster Kok

A Knot with Santa

Genesis

The Kraken's Mate

MURDER SPREES AND MUTE DECREES

The Trouble with Trying to Date a Murderer

For Recruits a Mute Boy

The Trouble With Trying to Save an Assassin

HAMMER AND FIST SERIES

Sledge and Claw (Hammer and Fist: Lextalion Book 1)

Inferno (Hammer and Fist: Geminatus Book 1)

RECOVERY ROAD SERIES

Forrest's #Win

Gentry's #Doms (MMM)

Jericho's #Switch (Sign up for my newsletter to get this one)

LOOKING FOR A BIT OF DARK EROTICA?

Jennifer Cody writes as Cinnamon Sin

Nefarius

Nefarius Too

Matty's Monster:

Captured

Tortured

Turned

Unleashed

Primal Prey:

Catch Me